THESE WORDS LEAVE SCARS

Jeremy Megargee

Curious Corvid

PUBLISHING

o you believe that literature can create scars? I do. I've been consuming books religiously since my youth, a ravenous cannibal for pages, addicted to the smell of old parchment and the taste of certain sentences on my tongue.

I've dined on all genres that the literary menu has to offer, and I have not entirely escaped some of these books unscathed. Words leave wounds. Phrases and thoughts and feelings bleeding off the page, bleeding into you, and sooner or later, you notice a gash in your psyche. It'll heal when you finish the book and replace it on the shelf, but it'll scar. A little crisscrossed remnant of a short story or novel or poem that left an imprint upon you. All the writers that are worth a damn seek to leave these scars. We want to mark you. We want you to taste the hurt that we have tasted. We want you to remember our words, and we aren't afraid to brandish knives in your brain to accomplish that.

I am as much a butcher as I am a wordsmith. I'm not afraid to cut you. If anything, I am purposefully aiming to do so. I want to slice and dice and slash and rend until you feel. Every short story in this collection is intended to tear into some part of your heart or your soul. The monsters come in different forms, but the intent is always the same. Show me your scars, and I'll show you mine.

A scar is a lovely thing. It is a testament to pain that was endured, and pain that was survived. It is the flesh art of the strange and the broken and the tortured. We all have our scars, and I'm eager to leave you with a few new ones.

Remember me when you look at them.

And know that I put them there.

- Jeremy Megargee, May 2025

CONTENT WARNINGS:

Depicts violence and violent tendencies, extreme body horror, cannibalism, generational trauma, extreme mental health disturbances, domestic violence, murder, eroticism, gore, and overall dark and disturbing content.

SHE IS CORRUPTION

The moss is endless, a king-sized nature bed that houses snails and isopods, but I've never been picky about my company. I sleep and awaken at hour intervals, always beneath moon glint, and time has lost all semblance of meaning for me. I'm in an eastern forest, but I don't know the exact geographical location. It's a place of virgin hemlocks, monolithic mastodon trees that tower above and make of me a human speck in comparison to their hundreds and hundreds of years of life. I wander, I drift, and that's all there is. I have no wife, no career, and no tether to the shiny bauble called civilization. It's just birdsong, cicada music, and black bear claws rending past bark and heartwood. No one speaks to me, and I've forgotten how to use my vocal cords. Maybe they've dried out, now just mummified husks somewhere in the bowels of the throat . . .

My clothes are tattered, my beard is tangled and unkempt, and my soul is a patchwork thing with no clear purpose. It's strange to go many years without interacting with another human being. We are social creatures, but after a while, you forget what it means to be a person. You revert back to what you are at the core, that hidden heathen heart, and that is an animal. A scared, hungry animal that forages for nuts and berries and scrapes up the remnants of carnivore feasts to roast over little campfires.

I've walked so long that the soles of my boots have split and the heels of my feet have become calloused, hard like leather, but it bothers me not. I like to feel the soil when I'm close to the dirt, I can place my ear against it and almost hear the pulse of the Earth. She's a broken, bleeding, hemorrhaging planet, but I'm just one man, and there's nothing I can do about that. So I walk old game trails that lead to nowhere, I watch mother deer teaching their fawns to walk on spaghetti legs, and when dead trees fall to crack the ground with their burden, I'm there to hear it, and I often mourn.

A daylight wilderness is a sleeping giant—listless, sunny, and prone to pretty wildflowers—but the night woods, the yearning, breathing night woods, they are what I crave, and there's a part of me that desires to find something there. I don't know what, but I believe it's more likely to be a *who*. I've listened to the coyotes howling and snarling over bits of carrion, family feuds that last for hours. I've watched the owls watching me, and in their eyes I've found an intelligent abyss that exists nowhere else in this world. Orchids that bloom white at midnight, vines that grow like serpents, opossums clinging to low limbs with pouches full of babes that gape and smile . . .

I'm in a daze when I walk the forests at night. I do it because no one else does it, and that suits me just fine. I've seen the things that swim black and large in creeks when there is no starlight. I've walked with rogue ungulates, hooves crunching leaf litter, and I've heard the grunts of their confusion at this two-legged thing haunting their forest, this man-wraith that should not be here yet is here, draped in shadow and something that rides the edge of sorrow.

I was a boy once, and I had a name, but I can't remember it. One day I left home and I took to the back roads, the clearings where utility poles thrum, until I finally reached a yawning mouth of tree line, and then the wild swallowed me.

I inhale the scent of pine, loam, and desolate spaces. The insects drink from me often, and I let them, because I know how difficult it is to scrounge up a meal. When you leave behind supermarkets and fast-food restaurants, you become fully aware of human frailty. You watch the flesh cling to your bones, and you see those deep-purple hollows that form beneath your eyes whenever you catch a reflection of yourself in unmoving water. From hearty and whole to scarecrow, and when the wind is strong, it often wants to take me with it. Sometimes I go along, letting it flutter me forward like a dead leaf, and it doesn't matter to me one way or another where I end up.

I am rarely hungry or thirsty; it's like my organs have stopped caring for such generic needs, but there's one desire that hasn't left me, and if anything, it burns deeper than ever, so much brighter and hotter than the cookfire that blackens my squirrel meat. It's a want of a different kind of companionship. An unusual, dreamlike tryst . . .

I want love.

I want something or someone to care, and there's this irrational gnawing in the back of my brain that tells me something out here does. I don't know what, or who, it is, and I can't comprehend the true meaning, but there's a partner in this wilderness that has waited for me for a timeless age.

I hear her sometimes at 3 a.m., whispering from miles far away in some black-shrouded grove where even the moonlight cannot reach. Dancing in a dress of leaves brown and withered, her hair dead witchgrass that curls to canary-colored points, and thin arms twirling, little more than bones and wasted marrow. There's nightsong in her heart, and affection patiently contained, waiting, always waiting . . .

"You can stay here. Past the lightning-pitted elm, through the cavern where the cave crickets leap, under the rainbow and in the land of forever sleep . . ."

I need her. She's happiness, and since birth, I haven't felt that. I think I'll feel it with her. I have to walk, I have to wander, and I have to search . . .

"Find me."

Days with bruise-colored skies, nights so starry that I feel exposed beneath constant pinprick light. Snapping twigs with footfalls, scarred lacerations up and down my arms, thorn-kiss remnants, the blood always flowing fresh when a new plant reaches for me with little hooked barbs.

I dream, but rarely when I'm asleep. No civilization to tether me, no bright cityscapes to play with my circadian rhythm. Just ravines, gorges, clearings, groves, and creaking forests full of nocturnal things that chirp and scream. A mother fox watches me from her den, the little ones within yelping when she pulls them from the tit. She' sleek and lovely in the starlight, and she looks at me with something akin to human pity. What does she see? What broken, lovestruck scarecrow walks in her woods, jaw agape in a bearded maw, pupils dilated, more floating than hiking? Her shoulders are hunched, red velvety snout twitching, and I can tell that she smells wrongness. The aroma of the brainsick damned. She waits until I'm out of her line of sight, far into the darker tree line, and then she slouches off from whence she came.

I hear siren whispers that drift down from the sky, snowflakes in my eardrums, and I know the mistress is calling. I see her in my head, contorted spine turned to me, all bones and bliss, a great pair of rusted shears in her long spiderlike fingers, and she is cutting at withered orchids, tending to her humble garden, a garden that grows so deep in the wilderness that it has not seen a human visitor for thousands of years.

Can you imagine that? Yearning for companionship for so long that you've dried up like a husk. You're a moth that never learned to fly, lips that never felt a kiss, a flower that died before it ever bloomed . . .

I can imagine. I've been so lonesome that I've hugged the dirt beneath me in an effort to draw some semblance of warmth from it, a bit of affection, and I've woken cold with centipedes nesting in my eyebrows. It embitters a man to go so long without love. Changes his mindset, brutalizes his headspace, makes him feel that he is the last of his kind and that he can never have what he truly wants.

No one to hold your hand and curl fingers into your hair while you're gutsick with a belly full of blackberries, not sure if you'll live or die, but too nauseous to care, so you turn your midnight-smeared mouth up to a sickle of moon and you beg and you plead for just a ghost of tenderness. That was my state the first time I saw her. She was in the moon, her eye a long oval, her mouth a crater, her hair spilling from a pitted, rounded face. She spoke poems to me as I clutched my boiling innards and hoped not to die. Each line was in a language older than the tallest virgin hemlocks, but I understood the sentiment, the tone, and the desire to connect . . .

I died as she spoke, or I thought I did, but it was just a sleep coma, and I awoke much later, and she had left with the moon. I felt hollow and thirsty, but healed. No longer lost, no longer caged by frailty of soul, but head over heels in love.

And love can drive a man to far, strange places . . .

The cavern passages loop on, ending in twisted chasms, and there are moments where I stumble and think I'll drop the torch. The sound of cave water constantly dripping takes on an orchestral quality in my head—the slow plink and plop of voices, each one whispering of long lost flames, soulmates that were never built to last. It takes days to navigate that underground world, and I camp in the cavern. It's like being in an enormous damp cocoon, and when you awaken and open your eyelids, there's only blackness to greet you, so it's hard to tell if you exist at all in such a place. Incorporeal, just vaguely sentient meat, and when I emerge into open night again, my lips are chapped raw and dying for a kiss. I know I won't have to trek far to receive it . . .

On a knobby hill, bathed in shards of moonbeam, there stands that lightning-scarred elm—branches of tortured limbs, trunk a hollow aperture, and the wind whistling through him, making his broken heartwood howl just for me. I don't walk so much as float, heels dragging on rich earth, and my heart begins to jackhammer in my chest because something tells me she isn't far, and that she is finally within reach after all this time. What is expected of a man when he meets his lover in dead midnight hours? Should he fall to her dirty feet and kiss them, supplicating all the while? Should he take her into his arms and squeeze her until her breath is his breath, and there's no way to differentiate between the two? Perhaps a bouquet picked along the way, of ragweed, of wilting daisies, of kudzu vines that tangle into each other, just as he forever wishes to tangle into her . . .

There's a path, rudimentary, and the trees are claustrophobic in this part of the wilderness. The canopies seem to reach for each other, branches like gnarled fingers, making the view above absolutely devoid of sky except for a few lost twinkling stars that manage to seep through. Trees that touch, roots that entangle beneath my feet, curling and hugging and wanting to be close. I scent the air, and it stinks of ammonia, pungent and difficult to trace . . .

I look down, and mushrooms line both sides of the natural path. Bloated, blackened, rotting fungal growths that serve as gathering places for clouds of gnats. They look especially fleshy, and I have to fight the compulsion to reach down and plunge fingers into that fruity and decayed organic material.

Ahead, much deeper in the hollow, come the first few notes of her nightsong. She sounds like sad owls, coyotes mourning their dead, insects that have flown their last, but beneath it all, past the façade of that funeral dirge, there is yearning that bisects human emotion. I relate on the deepest level, and I break into a desperate run, feet smashing through moss and fungus, hands knocking back thorns and vines, loping like a buck that smells a doe, and if a froth has collected in the corners of my mouth, I know in my heart she'll judge me not. The sharp parts of the forest open little cuts on me, and I'll be coming to her bloody, but there will be no shame in it. We all come into the world bloody, and where she waits is a different world entirely . . .

The thick overgrowth finally releases me, and I feel a percussive pop in both ears. It's like passing through an unseen veil, some shimmering barrier that protects just as much as it isolates. I look down, and I see that I've stepped into a fairy circle. Fat, thriving mushrooms create a sigil around me, and the air in my lungs turns saccharine . . .

A figure beckons from the center of the circle, and I go to her. I'm a bundle of nerves and insecurities. She's wizened, made fragile by her waiting, but she yearns all the same. The skull of a boar is affixed to her face, a death-mask threaded together with black twine, and she is cloaked in iridescent wings that flutter even if they've forgotten how to fly.

Her arms open to me, and they are the arms of elm, hemlock, oak, and willow, a daughter of the trees, and when her lips part, I hear creek water with the power to wash things clean, even a lost vagabond spirit . . .

Her words are an exotic maelstrom, syllables with no end, but she makes me see. She helps me understand.

"Beloved."

She is fae. The very last of the fae . . .

She is life. She is death. She is corruption.

Fingertips like gnarled roots graze my cheek, and she pulls me into her embrace. I take hold of her, this delicate creature, and the world that was ceases. We are seeds in the same pocket of soil.

She reaches down into the dusty chambers of my heart, and together, we begin to grow.

CASPIAN

The last mermaid glides through a poisoned sea, and she struggles not to let blood bubble up from her tortured gills. The saltwater is like black ichor, sludge from oil spills that have flowered together over the decades, and it burns to breathe. She twirls over dead gray coral, reef kingdoms forever fallen, and she tries her best to focus on the underwater road ahead. It is hard, but she must not lose heart.

Her name is Caspian, and she is dying. Her kindred are dead already, and extinction looms on the horizon. The merfolk will join the ranks of the Tasmanian Tiger, the Great Auk, and the Dodo. But she isn't dying alone. The oceans are dying with her.

It wasn't one thing that sounded the death knell, but many things. Endless pollution from an oblivious and uncaring human species, overfishing and the massacre of sea life, and the simple act of taking something for granted that was always there. The waters have turned from blue and green to brown and black, and bloated animal corpses float across the surface. She swims past rotting dolphins with their fins chopped off, victims of tangled nets and competitive fishermen. She flops over the gutted remains of a sperm whale baked to ruin in the unforgiving sun. She spins through rusted anchor chains and past archaic diving suits with skeletons inside, seaweed fluttering where hearts used to be.

Caspian's hair is the color of burnt copper, and a few weak surviving crabs nest in it. Her emerald eyes gleam in the deep ocean, but each day the twinkle in them dulls. Her shimmering azure scales are torn and tattered, and her tail fin is scarred so badly that her swimming trajectory always leans a little to the left. But even so—injured, sick, and close to the end—she swims for one last bastion of hope. There is rumor of a cove in the Mediterranean, a secret place where the water is clean, the ecosystem is thriving, and a few of her merfolk kin might have been able to flee and survive there. Her faith in that cove keeps her swimming even when her exhausted body wants to give up and sink.

She makes it another few miles, and then she has to rest. She paddles across the surface and reaches for the cracked shell of a sea turtle. Caspian hopes that the turtle might be alive and that they could share the last rays of the golden hour together, but within the shell there is nothing but shadow and the vague scent of carrion. Her frail arms wrap around it like a buoy, the dark waters lapping at her chest. She rests her cheek against the shell, using it as a pillow, and a part of her thinks she can hear the ghost of the turtle bellowing from deep inside.

The ocean is full of ghosts now, and they are the only company she has left to keep. Nightfall comes, and it is merciless. The cold comes with it, and it knifes through her. She dozes, and at some point, she dreams.

She dreams of jellyfish, manatees, and even mischievous sharks. She dreams of the living, and she dreams of the lost.

Caspian awakens to a harpoon whistling past her face, the rusted spearhead coming so close that it traces a single red laceration across her cheek. Her eyelashes flutter, flecks of salt tangled in her gaze, and she can just make out the ramshackle raft floating a few feet from her. It's a bastardized excuse for a boat, all splintered mast and mismatched logs, the sail stitched together from sealskin.

She catches her breath, a deep inhalation, and the turtle shell slips from her grasp as she fumbles into a defensive pose. Her chest hurts, and it feels like there are razorblades lodged in there. Pressure sores have developed along her gills, and each movement costs her something. But if these last few months have taught her anything, it is not to endure pain, but to push beyond it.

Her attacker finally makes himself visible. He shambles to the edge of the raft and peers down at her, his mouth full of mossy teeth and stinking breath that she can smell even from a fair distance away. His lower half is covered in rags, bits of otter hide, and a belt of conch shells, and his upper torso is bare and scorched to the point of unhealthy crimson by the sun. His face is a bald, blistered dome, and it has been eaten up by skin cancer, the black tendrils tracing across his cheeks and his brow.

There's a knife in his hand, the handle taped up and wrapped in cloth, and Caspian notices how the sunbeams reflect off the black surface of the blade. It is obsidian, volcanic glass of the keenest edge, and it's clear to her that it's an object he plundered from somewhere rather than created himself.

The pirate leers at her, shading his eyes against the sun, and his tongue slips out past his teeth to lap at his horribly chapped bottom lip. The tongue is dry to the point of desiccation, and it makes Caspian nauseous to see it.

"The Atlantic bleeds with radiation, the Pacific is so full of garbage that you'd think the landfills spilled into it, and in all the hundreds of miles I've sailed this fine vessel of mine, I have seen only the sickly and the putrid. Sea critters of all shapes and sizes choking on the water that used to sustain them. Ain't that ironic, fishgirl?"

He crouches down at the very edge of his raft, cocking his head at her, and he rocks back and forth on the balls of his crusty feet.

"So which is you? Sickly, or putrid? From where I stand, I'd warrant you're both. The reaper ain't far off. I'm gonna have to help you meet him."

She floats on her back, using her tail fin to balance herself in the water. The pirate is an opportunistic killer, and she knows his type. Violence is all they understand.

"Let me swim in peace, and I won't end you."

He clucks his tongue against his cheek, that foul grin retaking the cancerous flesh of his jaw.

"By the looks of you, you're swimming with a bent fin, darlin'. Can't pick up much speed with a bent fin. The fish markets ain't seen mermaid meat in many moons now. Truth be told, the markets ain't seen much fresh meat at all. It's all spoiled and verminous. Times is tough on land. Man eats man on land . . ."

Her breathing is shallow, and she steels herself. His boat has drifted close, and by the hunger and greed in his beady eyes, she knows confrontation is unavoidable.

"Don't you see? I'm your mercy."

He is quicker than she would have given him credit for. In a flash, he snakes a hand into the water and drags her up onto the raft by a handful of her copper hair, and he whips her body down against the splintered logs. He snarls and propels his arm downward, stabbing wildly with the knife, but she rolls to the side and avoids the blade as it peppers the wood of the boat's floor.

Caspian flips herself forward and wraps both arms around his neck, locking him in a sleeper hold, and then she allows her powerful tail fin to wrap itself around the pirate's torso. She is like a constrictor snake, squeezing him tighter and tighter, and she screams banshee-like into the sky. He is slashing at her with the knife, but he can't get a good angle. It scrapes against her scales, but it won't sink in deep enough. His tongue flops out, and his skin turns purple. His eyeballs pop blood vessels one by one until they're just bulging scarlet orbs in his head. He bites in desperation and accidentally chews through his own tongue, and it falls like a mutilated nightcrawler into the sea. She keeps squeezing and constricting, and there's a percussive smacking noise as both eyeballs burst from their orbital sockets and roll down his chest, the nerve tissue trailing out like octopus tentacles. The fight goes out of him, and his body droops lifeless against her. Caspian lets the man loose, and she falls onto her back on the boat. She coughs violently, and each cough speckles her lips with rose petals of blood.

Her emerald eyes look to the heavens, but there's no help up there. There is just the roiling ocean and the dead pirate and the agony that feels like fire in her gills.

She could give up now. She could take the obsidian knife and carve through her own windpipe, and the suffering would end. But she won't do that. She can't do that.

She will swallow her suffering, and she will get to the cove, even if it costs her everything.

She stays on the raft for a while, trying her best to focus on her breathing. Hours bleed into days, and she is lost in delirium. A wounded sea cow swims up next to the raft at some point, its big body pierced with harpoons, tangled in netting, <u>and</u> its kind eyes glazed over and rolling in its head. It's so full of jagged spears that it resembles a porcupine displaying quills, and Caspian draws on some of her energy reserves to roll onto her side and pet it on the smooth warm skin of its skull. It seems to appreciate this small comfort, and it swims next to her for as long as it can. When it can swim no more, it sinks, and she watches it fall down into the deep, a bloom of red swirling up as it goes. She cries, and the crying makes her chest hurt. She hugs herself, trembling fingers held against emaciated ribs.

Some indeterminable time later, a brutal storm rolls in, the wind whipping the sail and tearing it free, the water roaring and angry, smashing the little raft from side to side. All is lost in a deepening fog, and Caspian can make no sense of her location. The ocean rages, and she thinks to herself that it is entitled to its rage.

The little boat was battered so ceaselessly that it falls apart around her, and she's forced to swim once again. She goes under, and she tries to find placidity beneath the turmoil above. Progress is slow, but it comes. She listens to the thunder from underwater, and she watches the lightning strikes flash across the surface.

She feels a terrible emptiness in the sea and in herself. She would go deeper and seek solace in the trenches below, but factories have dumped so many concoctions of chemicals into the water that to go deeper is to throw yourself into a vat of acid. The shallows are polluted, but at least they're not instantly lethal.

How did it get this bad?

She doesn't know. Her dealings with humans have been sparse, but shying away from them did no good. Their actions found her in the end. Their actions find all living things in the end. She hid from their follies, and disaster birthed itself all around her.

She remembers the last time she held her daughter.

That sweet little girl with the magenta fin. Her face black with oil, her throat coated in oil, her gills smeared and worthless. All that blackness found its way inside, and no matter what Caspian did to try and save her, she could not pull it out.

She is starting to forget what the ocean looked like when it was blue. Each time she tries to remember, she sees only oil. Only black. Only her daughter choking and sputtering and clawing at her throat in that endless swirling midnight.

Caspian was born to the depths, and swimming has never been difficult for her. A mermaid is a ballerina of the sea, and speed and cunning is ingrained into the DNA of the species. But here, in this watery wasteland, she must fight for each stroke. Her arms are sore and her tail fin is tired, and there is the itch of lingering infection underneath her scales. She rode out the storm in the shallows just under the surface, but now she is afraid to dive too far, because there are noxious pollutants below and constant threats above. It is a gamble either way.

Her strokes are slow, and she takes her time with each bit of forward motion. She's passing through a ghost fleet, a section of open ocean where great ships came to die. This is their graveyard, and they lurk around her like ruined giants. There are little capsized sailboats, shattered fishing vessels, and enormous cruise ships that sit like sad Titanics with not a soul aboard to luxuriate on their decks. It stirs something in Caspian to see theses ships abandoned and in a state of disrepair.

It reminds her of humans as a whole. They were once grand, and thus their creations were grand. But they became too many, and they consumed and destroyed and doomed themselves. They weren't content to poison the land and each other. They had to poison the sea too. She carries the weight of that poison inside of her, and it is something she never asked for.

She begins to notice the hundreds and hundreds of seagulls that roost on the rails and decks of the forsaken ships. They're maddened with an abundance of meat, but most of it is decayed and sour, not fit for consumption lest the consumer perish too. As a result, they've turned brazen. They've turned desperate. And these desperate seabirds stare at her with lifeless black doll eyes, and they do not see a mermaid. There is no respect for the majestic legend or lore of her kind. The gulls see flesh that isn't yet corrupted, flesh that still breathes and moves, and they resent it. They want it. They desire to stab beaks into that sensitive flesh and sup on the hot blood that hides underneath, and so they come for her.

Caspian notices just a few brave birds at first, but then they begin flapping up into the air together, a starving flock, and they descend like small white missiles that stab and peck at her exhausted body. She flails in the water, swatting at them, and the seabirds continue to dive-bomb, making off with tiny scraps of her skin and her scales. The squawking is so loud that it threatens to drive her crazy, and she hears insanity in the birds. That is what this entire world has been reduced to. Squawking, desperate *insanity*.

She has no choice but to dive, otherwise they'll pick her apart. She goes under just a few feet and swims where their talons and beaks can't puncture her. They circle above for a time, screaming in frustration, wanting so badly to eat her and turn her body to feces.

Soon, the madness boils over, and the seabirds turn on one another. They begin to kill each other in the sky, and it rains blood droplets and ripped white feathers. Avian corpses flop down into the waters just above Caspian, and she shivers as she swims. More corpses. More death. More ghosts to torment her.

She closes her eyes and she just swims. She drowns out the havoc and tries to think of the whale songs that were sung when she was still a little girl. Those big beautiful beasts making melodies that would rival any human orchestra. She hums those old whale songs to herself, and she puts her hope into a minuscule box inside of her heart. It sits tight with her pain and her sorrow, but it is all she has.

She wonders if there are any whales left out there. It's been a long time since she's seen one that wasn't just blubber and bones floating with milky eyes. How does a living thing know that it is the last of its kind? And what must that feel like?

Caspian thinks that she knows, but she hopes it isn't so. Merfolk are hardy, and they are survivors. They lived through the crumbling of Atlantis. They lived through the submarines and the warships that would fire on each other and torch the organisms below without even realizing or caring about such causalities. Human nations have risen and fallen in the lifetimes of the merfolk.

She can't be alone. The thought of being alone hurts worse than her ribs, her tail fin, and her failing gills. She finally opens her eyes, and she's swum far enough out—the ghost ships are far behind her, and the seabird blood feast is at an end. Her body floats to the surface, and she flips over, backstroking and moving at a leisurely pace.

The sky looks bruised, and she never noticed that before. Maybe it's her faltering vision. She hasn't spent enough time looking at the sky in her long mermaid life. The clouds don't seem healthy anymore, and when she scents the wind, she smells smoke on all horizons.

It's like the world is giving up, but she can't do that. She can't give up. She is hurting, and the sky is hurting too, but she can't stop. Caspian fears that if she stops swimming, her body will start to shut down. The aches and the injuries will pile up and become insurmountable.

The cove can't be much further out.

Her eyes don't see so well anymore, but maybe it'll be blue. She hopes for blue. If there is one color she loves above all, it is blue.

Her skull pounds, her breathing is labored, and dizziness comes and goes. She swims through another night, and there's a full moon up there painting the waters in a sickly yellow luminescence. It's hard to think, so she focuses on putting one arm in front of the other and using her tail fin the best she can under the circumstances.

At some point, she comes upon an island. She remembers the island from years past, and it was populated by little fishing villages and a few rustic homesteads. The last time she came through this way and saw it, the island was green and thriving.

Tonight the island is burning. The trees are blazing matchsticks in the dark, and cinders drift up from the conflagration. The wind carries heavy black smoke, and Caspian struggles not to inhale it even from a safe distance away. There are shapes on the beach, vague shadowed figures moving in and out of the inferno. The people that used to live on the island. The quiet souls that settled the land and never made much of a fuss.

Many of them congregate on the beach, and they're spit-roasting each other above untamed campfires. They tear into the cooking flesh of their own family members. They slobber and fight each other over morsels of their scorched children. They chase and kill each other with sharp wooden spears, and the aroma that drifts out to Caspian from the island is like pork that has roasted too long in a woodstove.

They don't look like people to her anymore. They look like soulless things that have forsaken morality. All that matters is eating and surviving, and they're oblivious to their home burning down to ash at their backs. Based on how widespread the flames are, she doesn't think the island will last the whole night through. They are like the gulls. They are desperate. They are mad. They are crossing a threshold that cannot be uncrossed.

There seems to be a leader among them, a vagabond with a tangled gray beard that reaches down to his navel. Some of his body parts are charred, and smeared ashy warpaint decorates his haunted eyes. He carries a large ceremonial spear, and the barbecued heads of several villagers are impaled through the keen tip. Caspian is a mile out from the shore, but he spots her. His eyes widen like broken saucers, and when he grins, gristles of flesh caught between his teeth give his mouth the appearance of a meat grinder.

He begins to hoot and holler, pointing the spear out in Caspian's direction. He calls to her, and she barely hears his voice from her vantage point. It is the soundtrack of a mind twisted into irreparable ribbons.

"See her? A succulent one. Untainted meat. Clean mermaid meat. Wouldn't we like untainted meat on our tongues? Fetch her. Kill her and flay her and cook her until her juices sizzle on the fire."

He leads the charge, wading out into the ocean, and many of the people follow him, a few even bursting from the tree line covered in flames, burning and still pursuing her. They flop awkwardly into the water, and the tide smashes them up, beating them from side to side. Most of them scream and drown, but a few manage to swim in her direction, their eyes full of ravenous hunger as they swallow down mouthfuls of polluted saltwater. She is wounded prey, and she is being hunted. Is there no rest in this world? Is there no reprieve from creatures that want to do harm?

She pulls away and begins to swim with all the strength she has, using her superior agility to navigate the waves in a way that her human pursuers never could. They curse her and throw obscenities, a few tossing wooden spears that don't have enough velocity to reach anywhere in her vicinity.

Caspian focuses hard on getting away from them and putting that burning island behind her. She sputters and flails and feels like a rabbit with a fox on its heels. A few keep up the hopeless pursuit, and they drown themselves trying to reach her and kill her, their bodies filling up with seawater and floating facedown like detritus. Even when the threat is gone, she still maintains her breakneck speed, the mermaid equivalent of running for her life, panic making her heart hammer so loudly in her chest that she fears it'll explode.

After what seems like hours later, she dares a look over her shoulder, and there's no one left to chase her. The island is far off, barely visible, just a tiny glowing ember in a blanket of darkness. She wants to keep swimming, but it's so incredibly difficult now. That was the last of her energy, and a second wind has no chance of coming. She's weaker than she's ever been in her life, and the feeling is new to her. She flips onto her side, and she allows herself to float. She knows that if she sleeps, she might not wake, but it all feels like too much to endure.

The ocean has transformed from friend to enemy, and it offers her no comfort. It is black, cold, and utterly indifferent.

Where there was once an abundance of life, there is now a void, and she feels like she's floating in a hearse made of foul liquid.

She lets the cold settle into her bones, and she tries not to think too much. Her thoughts are muddled, and the pain is everywhere.

Is it worth it to keep going? Does she even have it in her to try?

Palaces of coral, massive skyscrapers of reef and rock, and schools of vibrant fish twirling through open windows. Her sisters play together, making giant bubbles and using an empty clam shell to play fetch with their pet squid. Caspian floats through the squid's warm ink, and she feels at peace. Her tail is strong, and the scales shimmer beautifully.

The water is pure in her gills, and she finds herself exploring a kelp forest, twirling and spinning through lush green foliage. The seahorses visit, and they dance on her fingertips. It's safe here. A sanctuary, and she likes the way the sunlight pierces down through the surface to dazzle her eyes. She parts the kelp like a soft curtain, and her ancestors are there smiling down on her. Merfolk of generations past. Her great grandfather and her great grandmother, all white curly hair and gentle wrinkled faces, wizened by saltwater and sun. She likes being here with them. She wishes she could stay, but she feels something pull at her. What is that tugging sensation? At first she thinks it's the squid playfully wrapping tentacles around her body, but it's not that.

It's pain. Pain pulls her back.

Caspian awakens from her dream, her body sloshing in blackened waters, most of her limbs numb, and a deep anguish in her sternum. She tries to breathe, and the inhalation causes a splash of bright arterial blood to splatter down from her lips. Something is torn up inside of her. Something important. She realizes this with a detached sense of acceptance, and she tries to flop forward into the water so that she can continue swimming. She manages a few strokes, but it hurts too badly. Her eyes are tired, and it's a great struggle to keep them open.

She sees a vague gray shape approaching from the north. It's slow, and is it possible that a shark managed to survive the pollution and the ruin? Maybe that's her fate. A gaping mouth of serrated teeth, and it wouldn't be so bad. It is better than poison. Fast and quick is better than painful and slow.

She squints with her dimming vision, and she sees a bottlenose dolphin. It's old and in bad shape, and it is blind too. There is only pink scar tissue where its eyes used to be, likely damage inflicted by some of the oil and chemical spills. It gently nudges her. Caspian feels its wet smooth skin that is a patchwork of scars, and she does the only thing that comes to mind. She reaches out, tremors in her wrists, and she takes hold of its fin.

And before she realizes what is happening, it is carrying her along in the water, towing her body beside it. It cruises confidently through the water despite the lack of sight, and it approaches a coastal inlet with a jagged U rock formation serving as an opening. Caspian can barely believe what she sees beyond that opening. Through the narrow entrance, the black polluted seawater creeps back, and in that little sacred circle is only sparkling blue.

The cove. She made it to the cove . . .

She releases the dolphin, her fingertips brushing against its side. It's the only thanks she can offer the old girl, and the dolphin swims off away from her, vanishing into the dark waters from whence it came.

Caspian feels herself fading, but she flops forward and swims the last little bit of distance beneath the stone arch, and then she's in that blue water, and it feels divine on her tortured skin. It is salve in her wounds, bliss in her gills. She looks around, hoping to see some of her own kind, but all that she sees are mermaid skeletons on the rocks. Skulls, ribcages, and delicate tail fin bones. But that's okay. It doesn't matter now.

This place was meant for her, and it's a good place.

She reaches out, and she lets her hands play across the surface of the water. It's clear, clean, and cool. It is tinted turquoise in the predawn light, and it laps against the parts of her that are forever broken. It is the last little circle of unspoiled ocean, and she knows in her heart that she is the last of her kind. There are clownfish swimming beneath her, and mantis shrimp crawling along the jagged rim of the rocks. Everything is colorful, and it's been a long time since she's seen that.

Caspian dunks her head under the water, and she opens her eyes. She sees a thriving world down there, so many healthy and vibrant creatures. They're confined to the smallest of spaces, but they are there, and that is enough. She surfaces again, and she uses her arms to pull herself up and out of the water onto the rim of rock. She begins to cough, and it takes a long time for her to be able to stop. Her body shakes violently, and it takes a lot of effort to roll onto her side so that's she's facing the water of the cove. She clasps her hands together and rests her cheek on them. Her breathing is a rattle now, and every moment that passes, it gets quieter.

Her thoughts are quiet too, just waves lapping through her mind, and she welcomes them. Her scales lose their shine, the bioluminescence within starting to flicker out. She lets her arm flop down, and her fingertips dapple into the water, twirling lazy little circles there. It's early morning, and dawn is breaking. The clouds are oppressive, but sunshine manages to pierce through. The rays find Caspian's eyes, emeralds that twinkle even as they turn glassy.

The cove is eerily still all around her. Crabs crawl, fish nibble on algae, and snails slither along the rocks. The serenity is heavy, and this is the sea that she remembers. The sea from her girlhood. The sea where she lived and laughed and loved and swam without ever having to think about a dying world.

She came out of the endless stygian black, and she found the blue. Caspian stares into that blue now, and she feels the blue settle softly against her soul. The blue calms. The blue beckons. And deep in that lapping turquoise, she sees the face of her daughter smiling at her.

Caspian draws in a breath, blood drying on her lips, and she sighs. With that sigh, the pain is gone, and she escapes the black.

The last mermaid closes her eyes, and she dies.

PRETTY PLEASE

[Cavers found a cassette tape in a deep unmapped channel of Whitlow Cave. The passage tapered off to the size of a pinprick and further exploration was impossible. The tape appeared to have been there for many years, and it was marked only with a smeared thumbprint and a tuft of hair connected to a scrap of desiccated human scalp. The following is a transcript of the tape's audio.]

It provided me with a knife and fork, and it instructed me to eat my children. I ate them slowly, the utensils clacking against my teeth, and my children were soundless in their unmaking. Malleable clay, but their pleading eyes said much, and the sight forced me to belch up bile halfway through the gorging of flesh that had come from my flesh. It gave me napkins, and I wiped the juices of my gutted sons from my chin, the gore streaming between my bare breasts and creating a River Styx that pooled somewhere in my belly button.

They crawled across my lap, bleeding things, stump limbs dragging against my sensitive skin, and I painstakingly carved filets from their warm living bodies, shoving those morsels into my mouth with mechanical obedience. It is a surreal experience to eat creatures that you have mothered, but it happens often in the animal world. I remember having pet rats as a girl, and they'd often eat their young, so why should it be taboo for me?

They were my brood of pinkies, and I made of them a banquet. I sucked down their bone marrow and twined the fork into the exposed intestines, savoring a spaghetti feast, twirling and shoveling bites into my mouth. And it watches me in this dark place, hands gloved in leather, calloused fingertips tapping together between its knees. It seems momentarily satisfied. The face floats above, tethered with string, and it's like a moon full of craters and veins. When it glows on me, I feel wanted. It's my tremendous pleasure in this absence of life to make the Moon Daddy feel good.

[Static, a sound like claws tapping out melodies on a solid surface.]

It chokes me for eternities, and loving fingers press permanent tattoos into the skin of my throat. There is no time here, and each moment my windpipe is crushed, it billows out and repairs itself. We have nothing in the deep pressure of this void but each other, and there's trust in that. I stroke its wrist when it chokes me, fluttery touches, but I'm never confident in the act. It's like trying to caress a god. I pour into it awe and yearning and appreciation, and the pores of my face spill out droplets of sweat, and usually I get to gaze deeply at its face before my eyeballs start to get lost in the red mist of subconjunctival hemorrhaging.

I weep crimson from the ruined blood vessels and stare up at it from a filter of plasma, and I count the imperfections of Moon Daddy's face. Gouges, grooves, and pockmarked places. I've seen it a billion times, and it's always special. No teeth, but it grins with gums, and they glisten purple when I've been an especially giving girl. Sometimes it lets me run a fingertip across the swaying string that connects body to head, and it's like charming a cobra during a street performance.

The body is toned, chest sprinkled with silver hair, and it wears a ravaged tuxedo open at the sternum from a time when it was something more or less than Moon Daddy. It doesn't matter here. We're all equals in our dismal depravity, and what came before is not important. We had lives. We had dreams. We were little animals on a blue ball in a jailhouse called society, and to come here is to be free of it.

This is a place outside of places.

I always hoped for a kind of hurt that would be forever, and I found it. It has touched all parts of me with gloved hands. Skin, internal organs, and shredded remnants of soul. I don't suggest that you search for this place. You won't find it. You have to stumble in, and once you do, it is over.

I crawl to Moon Daddy when I'm just slop and sinew, and I cradle its boots and kiss the scuffed hide. I lick my fluids from them, the stew of my unspooled form, and it sits and relaxes and gazes off into the deep stygian murk where there is absolutely nothing to see. I wonder what it thinks about when it meditates. I don't know that it thinks.

It is a hollow like a bowl, and it's my purpose to pour my absolute everything into that empty aperture. I'd hate for it to be lonesome. We always begin again when it starts to crave and want. I've never denied it, because the control is reassuring. It's always firm when it tears me apart, and I feel safe when it lets me rest my cheek on its boot and quietly rot.

We have our routines.

[Words break off into screams that last for several minutes. They sound wet, as though making the sound caused parts of the screamer's body to rupture.]

What defines a relationship? That depends on the individual. It comes down to preference and what you're attracted to. For me, I bloom with femininity in the presence of a dominant figure. I want to submit. I want to curl into the fetal position and give until I'm gutted from the giving. It's probably foolish to see it this way. Moon Daddy is an entity that can't be ensnared into the trappings of such a union. It sups on pleasures, but I know it doesn't have the capacity to love me. And yet sometimes I question that, because in this endless dance of desecration we engage in together, I see a certain fondness in a facial twitch or a glimmer in the cracked headlights of its eyes.

There's tenderness in the torment.

It doesn't seek to degrade when it flays and it flenses, but when it does degrade, it is because that's what I crave from it. It is unspoken communication, and I suppose there is a small deep part of me that thinks I deserve to have my inner child chewed up and spat back into my face.

[The woman's voice fades out, and there is the sound of gnashing teeth. Violent, passionate chewing. It lasts for sixty minutes.]

If I were to have spilled these thoughts in the life that came before the dark place, I'd have been branded a pariah. But it doesn't matter here. Matter has no matter. We are so removed from what is natural that I've ceased to comprehend the meaning of that word.

It spins me up like a spider prince, and it extracts the veins delicately from my arms and legs. It's a gentle process, and I'm permitted to watch those thin ropes of blue being plucked free of the meat house that I inhabit.

Moon Daddy twirls them around its thick fingers, making a child's game of it, a cat's cradle of blood vessels. The bondage takes longer, and it's always my favorite part. It uses the veins still connected to the soft wounds in me, and it ropes me up, knotting my limbs, wrapping my arms, and crafting a shibari sculpture from the contorted angles of my butchered anatomy. It hauls me up, midair in the mist of the void, and the artery that anchors me trails somewhere far above into unknown chasms. I hang and I spin, its fleshy doll, and I savor the bondage. For me, it's a womb. I'm warm, imprisoned in the ropes of my own cerulean-colored veins, a sweet sensation, and I reach a level of spiritual ecstasy that was never obtainable when I lived as a woman with a family, a conscience, and anything tethering me to what used to be. This is raw otherness, and it's better here. Moon Daddy has mastered shibari, and it makes me wonder if it was a part of its culture in another life. I know that's fallacy, because it couldn't have ever been a person. It's beyond even the concept of what a person strives to be. I think I just struggle to humanize it, because we are always comparing other entities to ourselves in an effort to better understand them. You'll never get it unless you visit.

[The plucking of dripping strings, a violin of skin degloved from muscle, and to hear it is to imagine a composer that sits cross-legged in a hidden abattoir.]

I speak to you now because speech is all that is permitted to cross the threshold. A voice in the dark. If you were given a visual medium of what occurs here, your eyeballs would boil in their sockets and roll out across the ground still steaming. But a voice is subtle, and it can peel without perforating. I'm not just Moon Daddy's willing doll. I have other responsibilities aside from just those of a mutilated marionette.

I'm the bringer, the tempter, and I want you to know that how you currently exist is just a forced construct. There's more here. There's worse here. Is there a tingle under the flesh? It's a blanket waiting to be thrown off, a flower that has not yet learned how to properly bloom. If you are one of those rare ones that seeks to fall down to knobby knees and beg a creature greater than yourself for merciless education, then you are most welcome.

If you look at people around you and see nothing in them worth relating to, nothing worth interacting with, then perhaps it's time to abandon personhood. That's what this is. Detachment from the herd. A rabbit hole that cuts in all the ways you fantasize about being cut when you find the gumption to throw yourself in.

It waits here in the nothing—leather gloves, torn tuxedo, and a moon-face barely tethered with string. It'll be the daddy and the master and the unmaker. It hurts and it helps and it saves.

It is the savior I sought.

[A sound like heavy cumbersome boots echoing in a chamber with no walls and no ceiling. Footsteps that pace in circles, because there is no place else to walk.]

I can't reach far into the world I used to know. I'm too far below. So if you're listening, you're special. And maybe deep in the unloved fibers of your heart, you know that you're meant to be here too. If you get lucky and stagger in, just know that we only have forever.

Moon Daddy waits on the throne it built from the butchered slabs of my hips, and it stares silently into lost fathoms. We take some time after each session. Aftercare is important. I gather up the spools of blue vein that I lie in, and I crawl to its lap, dragging what is left of myself up with me.

There is no acknowledgement that I am there at all, but then, like a colossus rousing itself from a dream, its heavy hand floats over and lands across the rawness of my scalp. It pets me roughly, stroking as one might stroke a cat that requires a little extra firmness. I sigh contently for Moon Daddy, and it echoes all around us.

[A deeply sensual exhalation of breath; it sounds like it comes from a mouth that is lipless.]

A part of you will have to die if you ever want to see us. It'll have to shrivel and shiver under moonlight until you're as weak as you were at birth. Only then may you beg for the dark place. This room that isn't really a room.

Put your fingers into your mouth and tear until you're incapable of tearing anymore. Keep your eyes upward on the black vista of the sky, and watch the moonbeams through lashes crusted with tears.

But most importantly?

Say pretty please.

THERE WAS ONCE A CIRCUS

My grandfather used to be a circus clown. He was young in the 1950s, when traveling circuses were all the rage. It's hard to imagine him young, because he is ninety now, and he is the only family member that I have left. Both my parents died in New York City during an interstate pileup. I don't like to think about that. I'm not sure if they burned or if they tumbled from the windows of their car like tiny blackened scarecrows, and maybe it is better not to know. I'm still only a young girl, but I like to read, and Grandfather says I'm as sharp as a tack.

I'm often scared these days. I think something is wrong with Grandfather's mind. He forgets things. He becomes easily confused. Sometimes he enters a room and can't remember what brought him there. I have googled what could be wrong with him, but they are dark words, and I don't want to give those words power.

The word that bothers me the most is *dementia.*

That word means that Grandfather's brain is becoming mushy and impaired, and it would explain why he sometimes seems lost inside of himself. It would account for all the weird things he has been doing lately. He is a sweet old man and I love him very much, but sometimes I don't even recognize him, and there are moments when he doesn't recognize me.

He seems fixated on the clown that he used to be.

There is a morning where I find Grandfather out in the yard staring up at the sun. His mouth is agape and his cheeks look grizzled and white with stubble. He is usually so good about clean-shaving, but lately he doesn't bother with a razor. There is a bright red bulbous clown nose on his face, and I don't know where it could have come from.

I ask him, but he doesn't answer. There's a little drool in the corner of his mouth and I wipe it away with a napkin. I think he would stay out here all day, but I take his wrinkled hand and lead him inside.

I make him sit and have some coffee. He comes back to himself an hour later, and he removes the clown nose and drops it into the trash. We used to have the most amazing talks, and he'd spar with me on all kinds of topics, telling me all the while that I'm smart as a whip and I'm going places in this world.

Now Grandfather is not much of a conversationalist.

Grandfather dances naked in the living room, wearing nothing but a pair of oversized floppy clown shoes. They are red, yellow, and cobalt blue. I am embarrassed for him. I do not want to see this old shriveled body jangling about like an abandoned marionette. It makes him seem too vulnerable, too frail, and it is nothing a granddaughter is ever meant to see. He doesn't even realize that I'm here.

He is in a different year, a different decade, and his mind hasn't caught up. I throw a blanket over him and usher him to bed because it is the dead of night, and the clattering of his floppy shoes woke me up from a deep rest.

I don't know what to do. I could call a doctor, but I'm afraid that they will take me away. I don't want to lose Grandfather. I don't want to become an orphan.

I wish he would call me by my name again. It is Mercy. He calls me by lots of different names now, but none of them are mine. Sometimes I am Lionel, Betsy, or Pearl the Pinhead. These names are ghosts from his past, but sometimes ghosts come back.

There is a doghouse out back, but we haven't had a dog in forever. We used to have a pug named Cerberus, but he died many years ago when I was very little. It is just a small sagging collection of boards and tar these days, home to cobwebs and occasional visiting wildlife.

I don't know where Grandfather found the black balloons. I don't why there are so many of them. I don't understand what possessed him to fill up the old doghouse with those ugly bloated black balloons.

I take a kitchen knife out there and I pop them all. The sound of them popping makes me shiver all over, and the cold doesn't help. I want to take Grandfather by his big lovable jug ears and scream into his face that he is not a clown. He has not been a clown for a long time. That part of his life has floated away, a black balloon caught in a night breeze.

But there is something at work in him that is making it resurface.

I t is some unknown midnight hour, and time is flimsy for me. All the days have been blurring together because I haven't been sleeping while trying to be a caretaker for Grandfather. I go up to the attic because I hear calliope music playing up there. It scratches out from an ancient phonograph coated in dust.

Grandfather sits on a stool next to an open trunk. There are bits and pieces of costume spilling over from within. He is dressed head to toe in a clown outfit. Frilly cuffs, fluffy red dots for buttons, and those damned floppy shoes. His craggy face is smeared in white greasepaint, and he wears the bulb nose and a smudged black painted grin across severely chapped lips. He is not a happy clown. He looks like the saddest clown to ever exist. His body sags on the stool, and he resembles a deflated balloon.

His hands are calloused and veiny, big busted knuckles with coarse hairs, and he rubs them together anxiously between his knees. There's an impossibly deep well of emotion in those haunted old-man eyes, but he looks more lucid than I have seen him in months. I can tell that he finally recognizes me.

I just stand there and look at him. I can think of absolutely nothing to say.

Thankfully I don't have to break the silence, because he does it for me.

"I was just a young kid when I worked for the traveling circus, Mercy. I liked being a clown. Never felt much like a job to me. You twist up balloons, make animals of them, and you sing and dance and be a goofball to make the kids smile. I never had much trouble being a goofball."

He smiles, and the single bare bulb overhead illuminates his dentures. It's not a pretty sight, with the black paint covering his lips.

"That place was a playground after hours. Booze, cigarettes, and even burlesque girls that could make your night extra memorable. All things a teenager shouldn't be doing, but I can't lie to you, I indulged. The circus never felt like real life. It felt like some other dimension cut off from normalcy as a whole. I can still hear that old rusted Ferris wheel squeaking through the night. I can see the carnival barkers in their game booths. Hell, I can even taste the funnel cakes."

His tongue slips out, and he licks his lips to moisten them. It looks like a worm desperate for a rainfall.

"There was a sideshow, Mercy. That's what I need to tell you about. All manner of oddities on display in that tent. Deformed babies in jars, called 'pickled punks' in their time. Betsy the Bearded Lady. Sailors with tattoos all across their skin, back when tattoos were a rare sight to be seen. Men with flippers for hands, and a surly dwarf named Lionel that would spit at you as soon as look at you. You'd often find him drunk and sleeping it off next to the cookfire."

It's hard to read Grandfather's eyes, but I see immense pain there. He's struggling with something. There's something in his soul that wants to come out.

"There was one little fella that I can't forget. He was called Pearl the Pinhead. You know what a pinhead is, Mercy? It's this condition someone's born with. Microcephaly. He had this shrunken little body and a small egg-shaped head. The brain inside his skull was small too. Intellectually disabled, you understand. He was dimwitted, but in his way, he was sweet. Usually he'd just want a hug from folks. Trusting, ya know? God, I wish he hadn't'a been so trusting."

Grandfather's voice breaks, and the clown hangs his head.

"All the circus folk used to tease and torment Pearl. He was easy pickings, you see. Weak and frail and never would fight back. He'd just take it. Everyone would make a game of it. How to humiliate Pearl today? How to build a good joke off his crooked back?"

The old clown swallows, and he lifts his eyes and meets my gaze. It seems difficult for him to maintain that eye contact.

"I wish I could tell you that I didn't participate. I'd like to tell you that I was the one who would step in and defend Pearl when people would do those ugly things to him. But that would be a lie. I picked on him like everyone else did. I teased him, I laughed at him, and I tormented him when I could. It's hard for me to explain why I did that."

He pauses, and I notice tears are falling freely from his rheumy eyes, cutting through the greasepaint.

"I felt an aversion for Pearl. In my way, I suppose I hated him. I never saw him as a person, for he was so vastly different than all around him. Just this little big-eyed freak with the face of a rat, and even though he wanted to give you affection and make you like him, that just made folks want to hurt him more. And because everyone tormented Pearl, it was less taboo, you understand? It was the popular thing to do. We all made a hell of this world for Pearl. And I liked it, Mercy. That is the poison truth I hold in my heart. I *liked* seeing bad things happen to him."

Those big veiny hands rub together with more vigor now, and Grandfather can no longer hold my gaze. He stares vacantly at the floor, and through the darkness, I see all those black balloons floating behind him.

"One night after the rubes had all left through the gates, we were throwing firecrackers at Pearl and making him dance. He was scared. He had this look in his eyes like he was just hoping we'd tire of it so it would end, and he could rest. But it got worse. Folks started throwing beer bottles down, and the glass shattered and cut into his bare feet. He just wanted to get away from it all. He wanted peace. So Pearl scampered off, and being as dimwitted as he was, he managed to squeeze between two iron bars and find himself a hiding place."

Grandfather wipes at his eyes, his fingertips smearing against greasepaint.

"He knew no better. He didn't realize he was in a lion cage until it was already too late. And this particular lion was an old broken male that wasn't fit to perform anymore. We'd just gotten a new young one that was kept in another cage across the grounds. This one here was retired, and as a result, poorly cared for. Lions need a ridiculous amount of meat, but this one was often starved. He'd get scraps and slop, the stuff you should feed to pigs, but nothing substantial. He was so emaciated that you could see all his ribs, and he had mange along his fur. He'd often get so hungry, frothing at the mouth, that he'd bang his head against the iron bars, maybe hoping for a charitable meal, or maybe hoping for suicide, I'm not sure which."

I suddenly have the urge to clamp my hands over my ears, because I don't want to hear anymore, but I tough it out. This feels like a deathbed confession, and I hate that Grandfather has chosen me to hear it.

"That starved brainsick lion got his meal that night, Mercy. I don't want to tell you about how he mauled Pearl, but I have to. How he tore him open like a bag and spilled his guts out for all of us to see. Those claws dug rivets into his face, and I heard his tiny skull crunch when those three-inch canines sunk down into it. He made a rag doll of that pinhead. And I wish to god he would have killed him before he started eating him, but the lion didn't, Mercy. He ate him alive. Pearl was still moaning for us when he was being chewed and swallowed. He was begging and blubbering and crying for a mother that he never knew. I stood there and I watched. We all did. We did nothing to help. Not a hand was raised to save that unfortunate soul. I think most of us were too shocked to move, but someone should have done something. *I* should have done something."

He is sobbing now, and it is the worst of sounds. I wish for his lucidity to fade. I wish for him to just be a confused clown with dementia again.

"Part of the reason I convinced your momma to name you Mercy is because when I had the power to give mercy, I withheld it. I watched something blameless die, and I lifted not a single finger to stop it. The next morning a bullet was put into that mad lion's brain, and what remained of Pearl was removed with a shovel. It was nothing but red brine and specks of bone. We buried him and the lion together in an unmarked grave in that field, and we never returned to that town. Each year we traveled the country, we'd skip it, because most of us would always remember."

He leans forward, and the pain and delirium in his eyes makes me flinch backward.

"Pearl had no family. He came to us as an unwanted infant, and there is no one left alive to remember him. Except this old clown, and now you, Mercy. I've held it in my heart for what feels like lifetimes, and now I place the burden of this memory into your heart. I am *sorry* for it. I wish it could have been anyone else but you to hear the telling of it."

He stands, knees popping, and that former look of vacancy and confusion returns to his face. His moment of clarity is gone.

"Where I am?"

He walks deeper into the attic, pushing through a sea of black balloons.

I let him go.

RUPTURE

I swerve, trying desperately to correct the trajectory of the SUV and avoid the pedestrian, but it's a losing battle. I'm fighting with the wheel, knuckles aching with exertion, and I feel gravity losing control over me. There's a sensation of weightlessness, and I'm aware of the vehicle tumbling through the air, performing acrobatics above the bustling Baltimore street, and then the shriek of tortured metal fills the interior. The seat belt bites into me like a living animal, choking off the lungs, and there's a tremendous forceful crack as the back of my skull connects with something firm. My limbs flail outward, a mixture of saliva and blood splattering from my mouth, hitting the windshield in messy biological chunks, and that shriek of metal becomes a slow purr as the asphalt of the road slows the velocity of my ruined Honda CR-V.

That dying screech of ragged metal is the last sound I hear. My thoughts are soupy, and everything is horribly sore. I'm upside-down, fingertips scraping against the headliner, and the blood rushing to my head doesn't just pressurize and stop, instead it finds an outlet and leaves my body in slow fat drops from the nostrils and ear canals.

I watch a little scarlet pool collect beneath me, fingertips brushing through it, creating tidal waves. It's warm, and that warmth makes me tired. My eyelids flit lazily to the windshield, the glass decorated in a myriad of spiderweb cracks. There's something wrong happening out there. People are running, screaming, and more automobile accidents are occurring at the intersections ahead. I don't hear the screams. I just see mouths opening, and cords pulsing on necks as it all happens. There are black shapes slithering through the throng of humanity, oily and undulating, bedeviling things that are hard to make out because of the shattered glass.

It's like watching a silent movie, and I'm soothed by the pandemonium. This must be a dream, so I'll sleep to awaken. Make this chaos depart, silly brain. My eyelids close, and the panic starts to deaden. It doesn't matter. I just need to rest for a bit . . .

The world returns minutes later, and it's excruciating. A severe cramp in my leg serves as my alarm clock, and it reminds me of the gravity of my situation. I grasp blindly at the windshield and manage to pull a shard of glass free to use like a knife to slowly cut through the seat belt that binds my torso. There's a thump as my body falls to the side, free of the tethers, and a shockwave of pain reverberates in all the parts of me that are hurt. I smell gasoline, a cloying aroma that is so strong it makes me gag, and I crawl like a child from a massive hole in the windshield, emerging from a tattered womb into what seems to be an equally tattered city. I manage to gain my knees as the glow of the stoplight above me paints me in red hues, and I finally have time to make the worst realization of all.

I can't hear.

There's a dull internal ringing in my ears, but nothing else. There's madness all around me, a metropolitan area that is eating itself, but it comes to me in a soundless panorama. My hands lift up to the sides of my head, and both ear canals are absolutely scummed over with coagulated blood from the car accident. I'm a bit of a hypochondriac when it comes to injuries and illnesses, always looking up the worst things on WebMD late at night out of morbid curiosity, so it takes me only a moment to diagnose myself. When my skull hit that hard surface during the accident, both of my eardrums must have ruptured. I feel all the symptoms: the pain, the shaky equilibrium, and even a touch of nausea. I've heard that ruptured eardrums heal naturally with time, and hearing returns, but right now when the wounds are still fresh, it's a terrifying experience. One of the most important of my five senses has been stripped away, and I'm smack-dab in the middle of something I still haven't even begun to grasp. What the hell is going on? Is this a riot, a terrorist attack, some kind of mass-shooting incident?

I look around, and pedestrians are running in all directions, clumping together in human mini herds, and there seems to be a theme of flight, the sense that they're trying to get away from something. One of these mini herds runs past me and I try to stop someone in an effort to communicate, but the runner doesn't even break stride—he clips my shoulder and sends me weaving across the street, and I have to grab hold of a streetlamp to keep from falling. There's a man walking in the other direction, much calmer than everyone else, his mouth smeared in red like he's been stuffing his face with cherries, and I notice that he's bringing his own hand up to his mouth and chewing on the fingers, snapping off flesh in flayed chunks, ravenous as he consumes his own digits. There is something dark and slick and lashing connected to his side, burrowed into the meat of his torso, weaving with his movements, but it's all a blur, because I don't linger to see more.

I'm running, the breath ragged in my lungs, fear rocking through me on the most instinctual level. I get caught up in a mini herd, bouncing around with other panicked bodies, and I stay like this for a few blocks, just pounding my feet on the street, eyes darting everywhere, hearing nothing but a flat void, seeing buses burning, office windows blowing out from tall buildings, voracious black shapes darting from shadowed corners and picking off members of the herd, making of them hosts, and I don't stop running until I physically cannot continue, my exhausted body breaking from the herd and flopping up against a pawnshop window. There's a large flat-screen inside, and closed captioning has been left on, so I'm able to read the words beneath the CNN news anchor's sweating, makeup-glossed face . . .

"The breach resulted from research samples being drilled out from hydrothermal vents deep in the Indian Ocean. They burst forth in the thousands, and some unexplained impulse drew them to the surface. Marine biologists have concluded that they're a new species of lamprey, abnormally large, isolated for millions of years in these volcanic vents before the cracking of the node. They're amphibious, able to survive on land and 'swim' through the air via a means of propulsion that experts don't yet understand."

The woman's face slackens as she listens to voices all chirping over each other in her earpiece, and then she continues with the broadcast.

"Eyewitness accounts state that . . . they whisper. They speak a dead, parasitic tongue, and these articulations bring out self-destructive tendencies in the listener. It's happening all over the world, and the chief report we're receiving is that they're driving people to . . ."

She pauses, unsure of herself, but forging on regardless.

"Self-cannibalize. Once this process starts and the listener has been acquired, they attach to the host and feed. It's being said that there's another element in play here, that these aren't just undiscovered animals, but something much more sinister, though we cannot confirm or deny these allegations . . .

We're urging citizens to utilize earplugs, headphones, anything to drown out the noise. Do *not* listen if you encounter these entities. It seems to . . . invite them to attach."

I've seen enough. Witnessing the almost clinical, traumatized detachment of the news anchor's face as she spoke these words has left me in a state of stunned bewilderment. Lampreys? Those ugly as sin, eellike things that attach to fish and suck the juices from them? I've seen them on the show *River Monsters*, but the idea that there are bigger versions of them causing all of this, deep-sea creatures that are able to exist on the surface . . .

All of it is almost too much to bear.

've made my way to the Inner Harbor, and it is like walking into the epicenter of an abattoir. My sneakers slosh through blood painted in violent red smears all over the ground, murals made of self-inflicted suffering. People are everywhere, each one a host, victimized by one of those lashing parasites. The prevalent sight here is chewing, and it is one nightmare visual after another. A businessman holds up his own shining dress shoe, and he gnaws on the severed foot that is inside, teeth struggling against the gristle of tendons. He grins as I pass, canines dripping plasma, and the lamprey attached to him caresses the back of his neck with its slick caudal fin, almost like it's petting him for being an especially good boy.

There's a wet smacking coming from the shadows beneath the Baltimore Aquarium, and I see it instead of hear it, a spattering of salvaged body parts. Men and women are in the process of disemboweling themselves and making slow banquets of their own intestines. They slurp up these snaky morsels like raw noodles, pushing them back into themselves after removing them from the abdominal cavity using nothing but fingernails and determination. I stumble away, struggling not to retch, and as I look out at the Patapsco River, I see all the decorative paddleboats out there, dragons and unicorns and fairytale beasts, and there are people sitting in them, people with midnight serpents latched on to their torsos, people scraping at the orbital sockets of their own eyes, digging the gelatin balls out with eager thumbs and plopping them onto equally eager tongues.

I'm surrounded by cannibals, and each individual is his or her own meal. My heel slips against a mound of miscellaneous gore, and I go down to my hands and knees at the water's edge, a hot stream of vomit bubbling up from within and spraying out from the splayed fingers that try to hold it in. I'm so caught up in the act of being sick that I don't even notice the little girl with blonde pigtails and a daisy-print dress skipping up to stand next to me. I look up, and I see a pudgy little hand pulling at the flesh of her cheek, dislodging handfuls of viscera and placing them into her mouth like bits of sweet candy. The gleaming bone of her jaw is already exposed on one side of her face, and I can't stop staring through that ragged face-hole at the nubs of her rotting baby teeth. Her lamprey is connected at the back of the neck, and it flicks from side to side in earnest, a giant tiara moving about her head.

She's speaking to me, and I scramble backwards and away, understanding nothing of her alien words but lip-reading the best I can.

"Aw, mister, you don't got one yet! It's okay, one will find you. Listen close when it talks, cuz it tells ya what it likes to eat. They're all different and got their own personalities, and they like different sweet meats. I named mine Penelope, and she likes cheeks, cuz they are rosy and good."

The girl keeps scraping at her face as she speaks, funneling more of her own lacerated cheek between her lips. She sucks at her fingers, licking what is leftover like dripping ice cream.

"They speak the dead tongue, the tongue of the trench, and they've been starved for so long. They're real hungry, mister. I thought eating my face would hurt, but it's nice, cuz Penelope makes it numb and warm, and it doesn't hurt at all. She told me she don't have the right digestive parts to eat me herself, so I have to help her. She is not some big predator like a lion or bear or something, she is just a parasite, and parasites need friends to feed them, so now we're friends."

The girl keeps rambling, and it is a silent horror, her mouth opening and closing, that gaping wound in her cheek pulsing from side to side like an envelope of torn tissue. I feel like a deaf person being subjected to a snuff film. No sound, just traumatic images . . .

"Don't cry, mister. You will make a friend."

She dances in a little circle, waving her hands around at the unspeakable acts happening all around us in the Inner Harbor. Cherry-colored droplets of her own plasma fly from her fingertips as she spins.

"See? Everyone is making friends . . ."

I'm forcing myself back up to my feet, and once again, I'm running, leaving that little beast of a child to consume herself. Endless masticating in all directions, the whole population of Baltimore settling down to a banquet of self.

The one mercy is that I can't hear the sound of so many sets of teeth chewing and chewing and chewing . . .

've been wandering aimlessly, just trying to find a part of the city that's still something of a safe haven. I'm new to the area and have only been working here for a few months, so much of it is still a maze to me, but I recognize quickly that I've stumbled into a bad neighborhood. I'm passing ramshackle rowhouses, crumbling brick walls tagged in graffiti, and streets that are strewn with garbage. I run into a few self-consuming cannibals along the way, but it seems most of them are drawn to the Inner Harbor, heading in that direction like it's a mass cafeteria. I see a sign up ahead, pockmarked with bullet holes, and the tangled trees beyond the entrance.

I've reached Leakin Park. Even when I first moved here, I heard about this place's reputation. A crime hotbed, and a convenient place for the local gangs to dump bodies. It's a filthy, secretive forest, and the locals refer to it as "the city's largest unregistered graveyard." Under most circumstances I wouldn't want anything to do with this place, but it's one of the few areas that offers a rural atmosphere, and maybe the lampreys prefer sticking to the urban neighborhoods where hosts are more plentiful. I decide to take a chance, and I stagger into the park's perimeter.

I walk past rusted guardrails, huge piles of garbage bags stacked up, and discarded tires flung from the rim. The road soon meanders into a heavily wooded section of the park, and I allow myself to become lost in the trees, bare branches tearing at my clothes and the skin beneath.

I reach the top of a ravine, and a powerful sensation forces me to drop down to a knee. My left ear has popped, almost like the feeling you get when traveling into another elevation, but the hearing is flickering in and out—a radio with a bad connection, bird chirps, dead leaves rustling in the wind, all those little sounds that those with full hearing take for granted. The damage of that ear's rupture must not have been as severe as I feared, because it seems to be abating, albeit gradually. I'm tempted to celebrate, but I become aware of the new sound in front of me, flickering back and forth, something that approached so subtly that I hadn't even noticed.

I lift my eyes, and I'm staring into a gaping mouth of hooked, hollow teeth, the keratin the color of yellowed infection, and the oral disc pulsates mere feet from my face, a hypnotic pull of horny plates and a pistonlike tongue. The lamprey is the size of a large dog, and it floats in the air, tail whipping from side to side, hovering there like a hummingbird from the blackest depths of the ocean. I'm reminded of an eel grown to abnormal proportions, and little translucent eyes on opposite sides of the thing's node of a head are locked onto me. The caudal fin is undulating back and forth, beckoning to me, and I can't help but think of it as a come-hither gesture.

The whisper struggles to break past my faulty hearing, and what I can pick up is a rasp, a trilling of vocal mimicry, and it makes me think of a lifelong chain-smoker speaking through the ruined remnants of throat cancer.

"Son of Adam, I have come. We are priests of the Maw, and a cleansing of flesh is a cleansing of self. Spawned in the dead waters, where even the great squids fear to dwell. Of you, I would taste. Shall you make a covenant with me? Invite me to dinner. We can be together forever, and I will sup on the parts of you that you hate and the parts that you love in equal measure."

The words trickle through a few at a time, and my partially ruptured eardrum prevents me from hearing them all. It's my only saving grace, because the thing has the power to compel. The lamprey speaks in a language that is as foreign as the lightless vents that it came from, but somehow my brain deciphers it into English. It quivers in front of me, and a clear-colored ooze of slobber drips from its mouth, a sign of anticipation . . .

". . . An honor to be accepted into the Maw. How can you ever fully understand yourself, if you are not permitted to taste yourself? The spleen will be the start. I scent it even now. Nutmeg, roasted pork, the raw texture of shrimp. Bliss to us both, and let it be the fostering of our union. Where would you like me to attach? The kiss of teeth, the bloom of connection . . ."

I become aware that, much like old vampire lore, I have to invite this aberration across the threshold, and I have to give it permission to attach. But I have no will to deny the lamprey, because I feel its influence working to rend my resistance into shreds. My hearing is returning to normal in my left ear at the absolute worst time, and more and more of these dark words are sinking in . . .

I will not fucking succumb to this. I will not eat myself.

I notice a bottle half obscured in the dead leaves, and my hand creeps towards it, the fingers almost operating against an invisible force. The lamprey notices, and it shakes itself angrily, a porcupine resentful that it's being denied.

"This is fated. Children of earth, children of sea. We are meant for each other . . ."

My hand closes around the neck of the bottle, and with a look of rebellion burning in my eyes, I shatter it against a rock. I bring the makeshift blade to my ear, and I grind it into the ear canal, carving into the rupture, making of it a waterfall of blood. It is agonizing pain, but I smile through it, because the trapdoor words of the lamprey are fading into beautiful silence. It senses this, and the last thing I hear is a cheated howl that bursts through that toothed maw, and before my grisly work is finished, the thing makes a slithering departure through the trees, seeking out a more willing host.

I crouch there on my knees in the leaves, plasma splashed against my cheek, the whole of humankind just a plate on the lamprey's table, but I've escaped this twisted Last Supper. I hear absolutely nothing. I'm aware that I'm breathing hard, but deafening stillness clings to me, and I find it peaceful. I relish the ruptures, because they are my salvation.

The emotion hits, a volcanic eruption of fear, sorrow, panicked laughter, all of it bleeding out from a traumatized soul. I might as well be a mime putting on a performance for no one.

The silence stretches on, and I am thankful for it.

RIP'S STORY

"You've barely touched your pasta. Is something wrong?"

Rip stirs like a man sinking in the black ichor of a marsh, and it takes a considerable effort for him to lift the weight of his own head to look across the long table at Lady. The dim candelabra flames play tricks with his eyes, and for the briefest moment, her face is all melted wax. He pinches the bridge of his nose and steadies himself, and when he looks again, it's the familiar face of the woman he lives with staring back at him.

Rip knows the features of Lady's face intimately, every curve, wrinkle, and laugh line. Her fine red hair, the blush in her high cheekbones like crushed rose petals, and the milky porcelain of her skin. Lips painted in the shade of rubies, and he can't recall if he has ever seen her without lipstick. And then the eyes that he spends a great deal of his time lost in—very black, very intent—and when he gazes long, he feels like an older masculine Alice tumbling between dual rabbit holes. The free fall is forever, and he can never find firm footing. There are even moments in Rip's life when he feels like Lady's face is the only face he ever sees.

"Sorry. Mind wandering again. The sauce is quite good."

He tightens his grip on the fork, stabbing down into the creamy crimson and bringing a mouthful up. It's a flavorful burst of tomato and basil, but the undertaste is hollow, lacking something essential. He can't speak on that. He dare not.

Lady watches him eat, almost piercingly inquisitive, as is her norm, and when she smiles, it's like her mouth cracks itself open. The teeth are glaringly white, perfect rows, and just a bit small for her gums so that a fair amount of pink shows.

"Old family recipe, a sprinkle of this, a dollop of that. A lady is entitled to her secrets, don't you think?"

She wipes at her mouth with a napkin, and Rip notices the smears of scarlet that remain on the pristine white.

"I'm glad you like it."

Rip often thinks that Lady could moonlight as a hypnotist if she wanted to. Her voice is a soothing croon, and all of her sentences sound like lullabies in the right hours of the evening. She makes him feel like a very old dog with weary bones, and she is the fireplace that crackles him down to sleep. He's lethargic when she's around, and she is always around.

"Maybe I'll have a walk after dinner. I could use some fresh air."

There's hesitation in his voice, and when he lifts his eyes to meet hers, there's fresh tension between them. She sits rigid like an agitated bird, tongue playing at a little canine to dislodge a piece of food.

"It's late and it's cold. There's no moon to light your way. You might fall. You might harm yourself out there."

Rip gazes at the window behind her, and it's a square of perfect fathomless dark. No starlight, nothing but inky tar. It's like looking out through a submarine porthole.

"All the same, I think it would be good for me. Stretch the legs a bit."

He chooses his words carefully, tiptoeing on eggshells and hoping desperately not to crack those shells underfoot.

"Your eyes are no good at night. Cataracts, I believe. You want to tumble into a ditch and starve? I'd have to haul you out, like a big lump."

Rip's brow furrows in confusion, and he uses his free hand to rub at his temple.

"I don't have cataracts."

"Sure you do. You've just forgotten. You are forgetful at times, Rip."

Lady uses a thumb to trace the rim of her wineglass, collecting the drops of red there to suckle off slowly. A new tone crawls into her voice, and there's an edge of constrained ugliness. The tone itself sounds like a challenge.

"Am I not enough for you? You have another woman out there you'd prefer to spend your time with? I shape my entire life around you. I sacrifice. I give until I've scraped at the marrow."

Black eyes, blacker than that window, and her mouth holds a curvature that seems to be deciding whether or not it wants to be cruel. Rip knows this behavior well. He knows how wise it would be to backpedal.

"No, Lady. You know that's not true. It's just that sometimes I feel trapped. I feel like a shut-in. I can't remember when I last took a walk, or even went to the store. When was the last time we visited a restaurant instead of eating in?"

She makes a sound in the far back of her throat, an exasperated sigh, and her fingers clamp tighter on the stem of her wineglass. She swirls the liquid within, creating a miniature chaotic storm of it.

"There's nothing out there but interference. I've sought meaning out there, and nothing fills up the emptiness. It's better in here. You keep me company. As far as I'm concerned, you are my world, Rip."

She leans forward across the dining table, her shoulders taking on a hunch that causes the straps of her tight black dress to bunch up.

"Don't you feel the same?"

His mouth falls open, one hand nervously stroking at the salt and pepper in his beard. He feels ineffectual. He doesn't feel like a man, or even a person. He feels like a kept rodent to be stroked when it is good, and punished when it is bad.

"Of course, Lady. You mean a lot to me."

She has lowered her head, not looking at him, and her lips have drawn tight. The light from the candle flames dance across the walls, creating untrustworthy shadows. Rip feels like a scared little boy that needs to prove himself. He has to work for affection. He has to earn it.

"Hey, forget I mentioned it. We can sit by the fire and read tonight. Maybe play that record you like?"

Not a peep from Lady's end of the table, nothing to indicate that she's alive at all except for the slow rise and fall of her sharp shoulder blades as she breathes. A flood of anxiety pours into Rip's body, and the silence makes him itch. She knows this, and she uses it. The silent treatment has always been one of Lady's favorite tools.

He's about to keep trying, keep supplicating, but Lady's arms pop audibly from their sockets, becoming not like human limbs but limp strings of spaghetti, elongating and flopping against the floor, her fingers just damp spider-mitts with too-bright ruby polish. The noodle arms ripple and undulate, perspiration standing out in droplets on the elastic skin, and when she lifts her head up to look at him, one side of her face droops low, malformed fatty tissue, poorly constructed wax, something trying to be human but not quite getting right. A beady black pebble of an eye stares at him from a gaping crater of red raw tissue, and she screams and screams, this petty banshee, and Rip scrunches his body up and tries to make himself appear as small and nonthreatening as possible in his chair.

"You will not abandon me. I made all of this for you. I hate you for thinking of leaving. I'll love you if you stay. I try not to hate, but you make it hard. You make it so overwhelmingly hard."

The words don't last, transforming into primitive articulations of anger and abuse, just screams from some deep guttural place inside of Lady. Rip clamps his eyelids tight and wishes for it to stop. He wishes to be elsewhere, to be anything other than what he is.

He wants so badly to leave, but he doesn't know if he has the strength to. It's already been so long.

Rip sits on a futon, nestled into satin cushions, and Lady is cuddled up against him in tight, smothering proximity, her fingers twirling at the curls that taper down the back of her neck. The needle scratches at a record somewhere in the parlor at their backs, but neither of them seem interested in resetting it.

"It hurts when we fight. I never want to. I love you so much that it makes me shake sometimes. I vibrate from the inside out. I get worked up. You understand, right?"

Lady licks her licks after speaking these conciliatory words. Rip's hand rests like a dead fish on her thigh. She doesn't feel like a woman. She feels like warm plastic underneath his fingertips. There's a frenzied motion below that milky layer of skin, and he doesn't want to think about what that means.

"You're my medicine. When you're close, I feel better. I never like to yell. I think I yell because I know you're my soulmate, and it makes me ache. I feel so much sometimes. It's almost unbearable."

She's drinking him in with hungry black eyes, and her fingers dance upward to graze against the growth on his cheeks. Lady nuzzles closer, rubbing her head against him like a contented feline.

"You're a beautiful man. Handsome, strong, and loving. I love your arms, your jaw, and even the little tufts of gray in your nostrils. There are moments when it makes me sad that I can't crawl up inside of you, because then we'd be even closer."

Rip stares out of the window at the everlasting dark. Lady is always like this after one of her outbursts. She seems to realize on some dim level that her behavior has been horrible, and she tries to walk it back and overcompensate. She overloads his system with affectionate words and physical touch, telling him that she's sorry, that wasn't really her, and it'll never happen again. But it always does. Her behavior never changes long-term. It is theater between them, and because Rip can think of no other course of action, he plays along.

"Does it ever feel to you like it's always night here, Lady? It seems like there's never sunshine. No birds and no flowers. Where has the daylight gone?"

Rip reaches out and touches the condensation on the inner glass of the window. It's impossible to see anything of the exterior beyond the house. Pitch black nothingness.

She laughs, and it's like little pieces of glass shattering. It causes a shudder to travel through Rip's body, and he's sure she feels it, but she makes no comment.

"Silly ol' Rip. I see sunlight every day when you look at me. We have all we need here. Fulfillment. No reason to yearn for anything else."

He feels numb, and he doesn't know what to say. There's a part of him that believes that he shouldn't be here. Locked in something unnatural and detrimental to his being. When Lady speaks again, the words come out flat and discordant. Almost like the elaborate housewife role that she plays for him ceases to exist in that moment.

"There is nothing worse than *alone*. I think I'd do just about anything to never feel that again."

Rip doesn't doubt for even a second that she means it.

*Y*ou *ugly ungrateful bastard. Look what you make me do.*"

Rips stands in one corner of the kitchen like a shamefaced boy, picking at the skin around his fingernails as the anxiety eats up his insides. Lady's in front of the refrigerator, and she's gone temporarily mad again, the shift coming from something as innocuous as him folding the bathroom towels in a way that she didn't like.

She's smashing her face against the refrigerator door, loud percussive bangs, and each time she connects, her head flattens outward like a pancake. Something leaks from her ears and her nostrils, and Rip knows that it must be her blood, but it doesn't look or smell like blood. There's no iron scent to it, and it has the coloration of grimy yellow pus. Lady's neck flops back and forth, and her movements defy what the human frame should be capable of. She appears like a boneless marionette full to the brim with uncontrollable rage.

"I'll kill myself. I'll open my belly and throw my guts onto the walls. I don't deserve this."

"Please stop, Lady."

"You're so fucking stupid, and you never listen. Where's your brain? Were you born without it?"

Rip can hear the pathetic pleading in his own voice, and he'd drop to his knees and weep out apologies if only it would make her stop busting her face against the cold white appliance.

"I'm begging you to stop!"

She yanks open the freezer door, and she dumps a tray of ice cubes out into her hands. She takes the handful of cubes and begins to scrub them across the skin of her face, irritating the pores, forcing a brutalized rash to spread across her cheeks, nose, and brow. She hammers the ice cubes against her bared teeth, trying to break the enamel, but the ice breaks first, chips flying in every direction in the modest kitchen.

"Are you going to act right, Rip? Are you going to listen?"

"Yes. I promise. I made a mistake."

Fear and confusion puddles inside of him, and his soul feels soaked like a heavy sweater left out in the pouring rain. It's a familiar feeling with her, and he has felt it a thousand times before.

A montage of abuse, and since time doesn't feel linear here, Rip loses track of the hours and the days. It unusually starts with verbal degradation, Lady tearing down his character and the way he does things, vile insults thrown from painted lips, the spittle from her mouth always burning just a little if it comes into contact with his skin, like somewhere deep within her, there's a reservoir of battery acid.

Feigned apologetic charm when the explosions are finished, just sugary sweet deceit that he's heard more times than he can count. *I didn't mean it, Rip. I lost control, Rip. I love you more than I love myself, and I'd never hurt you.*

But she does hurt him. She's hurting him now.

She's strangling him with one hand, fingers feeling wet and pulpy wrapped around his windpipe, the bones in her back and shoulders all out of position as she leans deeper into him, her eyes burning like coalfire, her mouth a rotten rictus, and she drags questing fingers across the cutting board and takes up the flensing knife.

Rip struggles for breath, lungs full of invisible nails, and phantom trilobites are starting to swim across his vision.

"This is your fault. You make me do things."

She piles all of her unpredictable caustic emotions atop him, smothering him with dark feelings that she seems to have an inability to regulate, and this suffocates just as much as the fingers that dig into his throat.

Lady positions the tip of the knife along his groin, the blade kissing up against the denim of his jeans.

"I could take *it*, Rip. It's mine to take."

Her hand lowers, and she unzips his fly, allowing the knife free entry to slide into that opening, nothing as a barrier now but the thin material of his underpants.

He realizes at his core that she believes what she is saying. Lady doesn't see him as a partner. He is a possession for her to do with whatever she wills. He stares up at her, trembles radiating throughout his body, and he accepts that he is terrified of her, and has been for what seems like ages. No one could ever imagine what goes on behind closed doors with Lady. But is there anyone else is this whole fucking oppressive universe aside from the two of them? He's starting to think that there isn't.

The knife withdraws, and it clatters down to the floor. She's rising, hand letting loose from his throat, and she hisses in frustration and tears at her own locks of hair, looking like a Medusa tormented by maladaptive serpents.

Lady retreats to the bathroom, and the door closes. She'll sulk in there for a time and do whatever it is that she does to come down from an outburst. This is her pattern, this is her way.

Rip wishes he could tell someone about what happens to him in this house.

There is no one to tell.

Rip stands at the front door, hand grasping the brass knob. His palm sweats, and he doesn't make a move to turn the knob just yet. He wants to feel it, to know that it's there, to understand that it is within his power to twist it and open the door. But it's hard. The unfamiliar is out there. The unknowable drifts beyond these walls.

There's the addiction to think about. He's bonded to Lady through shared trauma, and to give her up seems akin to purging heroin from his veins. He knows it'll be painful. He knows he'll shake and be sick before it's all said and done. He's been with her for years. He doesn't know how their relationship even began. One day, it just *was*.

"Don't go."

He doesn't rotate his body or take his hand from the knob. Instead he simply cranes his neck and looks back at her over his shoulder.

"Please. I have no one. I'll be better."

"You always say that, Lady. You ask me to forgive you. You say it'll stop, but it never does."

His voice sounds soft and uncertain in his own ears, but he feels his resolve hardening deep in the heart.

She chokes back something that sounds like a blubbered sob. Her hair looks very straight in the light from the candelabras, almost artificial. A part of her chin starts to sag downward to the left, and she pushes it back into place, like she's readjusting a mask.

"We've been together for twenty years. You can't just throw that away. I remember when you were lost, swirling in the outer dark. I found you, and I cradled you close. I'd been lonesome in the black for longer than you could ever know. You gave me purpose . . ."

She takes a step closer to him, and her knee joint pops to the side, a jangled movement that looks wholly unnatural. She has to concentrate to straighten out the limb, her empty aching soul-black eyes imploring him to see her side of it all.

"I dressed myself in skin that I thought you'd like. I built us this house in the stygian void. Even though this flesh makes me itch, I stared into the mirror, trying new facial expressions for you. I learned how to be a woman. It's all been for *you*. Every bit of it."

Rip casts his eyes to the floorboards. He's not a stupid man, and he's been around her manipulations for so long now that it makes him nauseous to see her try to pull his strings like he's an obedient puppet.

He looks at her. He truly takes time to see Lady for what she is. Dysfunction and narcissism embodied. A pitiful void wearing a suit of poorly tailored flesh.

"You're not a person, Lady. I don't know what you are, but I know how you make me feel."

She sinks down to both knees, and there's a damp plop sound when her muscles connect with the floor. Mascara bleeds down from eyes desperate to replicate personhood without having any genuine understanding of what nourishes the human soul.

Lady's hands clasp together in mock prayer, and she begs.

"Don't open the door."

The longer he looks at her, the more her camouflage slips. Her skin splits into fissures, something comparable to plastic under pressure, and it's like she's molting. The woman-husk falling away, nothing but a crinkled carapace, and a long hairy insectile leg waves weakly in the air from a dark crack between her breasts.

When she speaks once more, it is barely even intelligible. More like a chitter than actual words.

"Please, don't wake up."

Rip decides not to spare Lady's unbecoming another glance. He opens the door, and he walks into the black. There are old mossy stone stairs in the open nothingness, and they lead somewhere.

He makes the decision to climb.

There's a dry choked gasp, and it takes Rip a few moments to realize that he made that sound. His body feels weak and atrophied. A massive unkept beard decorates his face, and it itches. The sound of beeping machinery brings him fully round, and his nostrils flare, picking up a sterile aroma that is always present in hospitals.

Two nurses burst into the room at the same time, and they both wear expressions of shock on their faces. The young women exchange a glance, and the one with the auburn hair is the first to tentatively step forward to his bedside.

"Mister Van Winkle, can you hear me?"

His eyes feel weak in the sockets, but he manages to turn his head and look at her.

"I'm sore and foggy. That feeling you get after a long sleep."

The nurse is looking at him like he's a modern marvel, and it takes a minute for her to even formulate a reply.

"I don't want to alarm you, sir, but that is to be expected. You've been in a coma for twenty years."

Rip isn't surprised. If anything, certain things make more sense now. On some level, maybe he always knew.

"I remember. I was in the black. It was tough to let go of things there. One of the hardest things I've ever done in my life."

He reaches a shaking arthritis-racked hand from the bed, and the young nurse leans down and takes hold of it. A small act of real human comfort, and it is something he's been starved of for twenty long years. The tears come quietly, and he lets them. They wash away a part of him that is better to be forgotten in the black.

Rip Van Winkle manages a half-smile.

"I'm glad I left."

Krieg wipes his fingertips across the condensation on the mirror, and he barely recognizes what looks back. Bottle blue curls, shifty hazel eyes, and that Cupid's-bow mouth that has always gotten him into trouble. He's never had a stable sense of self. He can't tell if he's pretty, or handsome, or some swollen abomination belched up from a sewer grate. He just *is*, and sometimes he wishes he wasn't here at all. Maybe that's why he's standing alone in this rest stop bathroom, a break from riding aimless across the interstates of the night. But that's not entirely honest. He knows where he's going. He's going to Ohio, and from there, he's going between a man's teeth.

If all goes according to the exchanged messages, he's going into a man's stomach. He's going into the void. Krieg will cease to be, and there's some semblance of softness in that. The knuckles of this world have busted him open more times than he cares to count, and it'll be a welcome experience to bleed on his own terms for once.

He met Montgomery using Tor. For the things Krieg likes, the things he wants, those long dark unspeakable things, you can't pussyfoot around on the surface of the internet. You've gotta go into the deep places, those subterranean pits of cyberspace where ugliness is celebrated and all the best knives are just waiting to cut.

That's where Montgomery waited, haunting a lonely message board like it was an empty room, biding time for the proper visitor. Krieg has been around. He's explored the smoky kink dungeons, and he's felt the sting of floggers ripping his flesh down to ribbons, the cold metal cock cages meant to emasculate, and the hulking sweat-soaked leather daddies that choked the air from his throat while whispering degradation into consenting ears. There is no sensation that has eluded him, save one. That unspoken desire. The final-frontier desire. It's something he's always struggled to phrase, a collection of words that represent coffin nails, a grisly, gruesome, and undeniably intoxicating *end*.

Krieg never thought anyone would get it, but to his pleasant surprise, Montgomery did. He sent pictures to Krieg—crew cut, thin glasses, and a square jaw. Conventionally attractive in the right light, but not remarkable. He wouldn't even usually be Krieg's type, but it's how receptive he was to the ultimate fantasy that sealed the deal.

The messages turned him on. Krieg felt a stiffening of both flesh and soul. The inappropriate and downright deranged course of the conversation made him swoon in ways that he has never allowed himself to swoon before.

He supposes the original fantasy was born of innocent knife-play sessions. The kiss of that steel, the sharp edge dragging and teasing and threatening to break the skin. Those moments always ended in a lack of fulfillment for Krieg. He craved a true carving. A flensing of tissue, to be shaped in the way of deli meat, made not a person with thoughts, but a pile of glistening organics.

Krieg hunted the dark web, seeking a butcher and an eater, and in Montgomery, he found both.

The man of his dreams. The man to kill him, eat him, and let his dreams digest in the hollow serpents of intestine. That man lives in Ohio, and that is where Krieg is going tonight.

Krieg drives with the windows down, hair wild and tangled, eyes caffeine-blasted and full of nocturnal yearning. The cold shocks his lungs, and he likes it. He also likes the slow rumble of the cherry red Miata as it tears down lost highways. The paint on the car is flaking, ruined by the years, but that doesn't matter anymore. Soon the vehicle will belong to no one.

He reaches forward and turns up the radio. Old emo tracks from his youth are playing. Pure nostalgia floats through his bloodstream. He remembers sloppy teenage make out sessions with endless angst-filled songs playing in the background.

The stark memory of discovering masturbation for the first time comes back. The vast basement with the mattress on the floor and the bare cinderblock walls. Touching himself slowly while flipping through a textbook about the Donner Party disaster. Those old sepia-tone photographs of the Sierra Nevada mountains, acres of woodland, and the mental visuals of charred human meat, scraps of bone scattered among cinders, and chewing teeth stained in red.

It was the chewing that made him climax.

Krieg smiles, lost in memory, lost on roads to nowhere.

But he knows in time, he'll find his somewhere. He's meant for the belly of the beast.

Montgomery carefully unfurls the sheet of plastic and drapes it over a sturdy oaken table. He affixes the ends with care, something bordering on tenderness, because that has always been his way. Vines choke inward from shattered windows, and ancient industrial furnaces watch him work with a malevolent stillness that has lasted for decades.

This abandoned factory is a vast chasm of liminal space with enormous drab moth-eaten curtains hanging down here and there, dishwater brown, the color of shit left too long in the bowl. Twisted girders, sagging floorboards, and the scent of rust. Montgomery breathes deeply of the aroma of oxidation, and it brings a warm smirk to his face.

He is a man at home in rust and dust.

He has chopped off and eaten pieces of men before. Small and inconsequential parts, mostly. Never taken by force, but given willingly, for consent is king in his heart. Usually the parts of them he finds most attractive. An earlobe here, a ring finger there, and once a thick flank steak cut from the curve of a Haitian lover's buttocks. They gave because it pleased him for them to give. He looked into them, those lost holes of need and yearning, puppies with lolling tongues, aching for approval, aching simply to ache, and it was their chosen privilege to lean into his blades.

It will be different with Krieg. More at stake, and on a much deeper and violently intimate level. When the stranger confessed these fantasies through text messages, Montgomery found himself hopelessly enamored with the idea.

For too long now he has contented himself on shallow cuts and mediocre appetizers. Stirring his hunger into life, but never satiating it with transformative meaning. He's done with bush-league mutilations. Montgomery wants an execution, and with it, a banquet. He wants a special friend to sit dead and dismembered in his tummy for a much longer duration.

His tongue slips out and moistens dry lips. He checks his watch. Krieg is coming.

His food is delivering itself.

Krieg rolls past the old rickety sign that reads Helltown, Ohio. Fitting. Just a name on a map, but his destiny is draped in the infernal. It doesn't take long to find the back road, pitted and forgotten, winding through woodland before arriving at grim smokestacks, torn ivy-threaded chain-link fencing, and the looming edifice of the derelict factory they chose to meet at.

He kills the engine and gets out of the car, simply standing there for a moment. There is no rush for what comes next. Krieg slips a cigarette from the crumpled pack in the back pocket of his jeans, and he lights up, gnats clouding around the little flame. His ember burns, and he drags, staring up at the last building he'll ever walk in to. It's a dead ragged dragon, all of its fire spent, and what remains is ash, tarnished metal, and windows like broken stye-encrusted eyes. There are no good intentions in those eyes. The place says, "Come-hither, explore me, and find the finale you never even knew that you needed."

The willing victim stares back. His own eyes are somewhat soulless. Not much there. A twitching masochism, and behind that, black stars that have lost their shine for no discernable reason at all. Krieg doesn't know why he wants this.

He just does.

And so he drops the cigarette, snubs it out beneath his heel, and into the dragon he goes.

The old machinery room that Montgomery chose is like a cathedral. Massive domed ceiling, industrial pillars at random intervals through the space, and as Krieg walks through it, footsteps echoing, he cannot help but feel the weight of his own mortality.

The man he chose waits for him. The god of his unmaking. Montgomery stands with his hands clasped in front of the plastic-covered table. He wears white slacks, white dress shoes, and a white cotton shirt open at the throat. His glasses are clean, not a smudge on either lens, and his facial expression would best be described as demure. His irises are black behind the glasses, clotted in shadow.

Krieg stops a few feet from his unmaker and places his hands deep into his pockets. "This place is nice. Makes me feel small and safe."

"I'm glad. I want that for you. I want it to be gentle until it's not. Soft until it's not."

Krieg looks around, his tongue scraping up against his teeth.

"A part of me thought you wouldn't think I was serious. That maybe it was just some roleplay. Others have thought that. That I wasn't serious."

"I imagine that was disappointing for you."

"Yeah. This is just what I need. I was born for it, you know? Like I hear it whispering sometimes in my bones."

He sighs, and he studies Montgomery's face. There isn't much in his expression but shadow and openness.

"Do you believe that some people are born to be butchered? Lambs seeking lions?"

Montgomery lifts his hand and brushes his thumb across the cleft in his chin.

"I think we all have destinies. Maybe this is yours. I think it's beautiful what you're doing. Ultimate submission. The wholesale sacrifice of flesh."

"Will you eat all of me?"

"All that I can. I'll make broth from the bones, and mincemeat from the scraps. The Plains Indians believed that every part of the sacred buffalo should be consumed or used. Waste nothing."

Montgomery steps closer to Krieg, closing the distance. The other man has dropped his chin, but Montgomery takes it and lifts up his head, gently caressing his cheek. He leans in and kisses him heartily, little specks of saliva leaving both men's lips as the kiss finally breaks. Krieg likes how soft Montgomery is. Tender. Painfully tender.

"You will not be a waste."

"Thank you. Would you like to me to disrobe?"

Montgomery steps back, giving him a bit of space, and gestures broadly with both hands.

"Please."

Krieg pulls his shirt from his torso and drops it to the floor, and then he carefully unbuckles his belt and starts yanking his jeans down his legs. He kicks off his boots and pulls the socks from his feet, noticing the cold for the first time. He hesitates for only a moment before hooking his thumbs into his underwear and removing them.

Once nude, wholeheartedly vulnerable, Krieg lowers himself down to both knees on the factory floor. Shoulders hunched, hands palms-up on his thighs, a pose of supplicating masochism. Submission to Montgomery.

He dares to cast his gaze up, staring at his unmaker. He is crying, but no sound leaves his throat. Every cell in his body is aroused. Krieg feels alive in a way that he never has before.

"How will you start?"

"I'll follow your instructions."

Montgomery reaches behind his back, and he retrieves a meat cleaver and a boning knife from the tabletop, holding them in both hands a few inches from Krieg's face.

"I'll slash your wrists. I'll make voids of your eyes. Just like you wanted."

Krieg smiles up at him. There's fate glimmering in his tear-drenched expression. Yes. That is all he's ever wanted.

"You have my full consent."

Montgomery answers with a swing of his arm. When the cleaver splits Krieg's face in two, he doesn't even feel it. Still smiling as blood-speckled teeth roll down his chin to rattle onto the factory floor.

After it is over, Montgomery's fine white clothes have been baptized red. His heart sings, his balls are empty, and his belly is full. Krieg feels good inside of him. Hearty, flavorful, and spiced in fulfillment. He carries the leftovers in a burlap sack, and not a single piece of meat will be discarded for scavengers.

His teeth are smeared red-black, and he whistles as he walks. He rubs his bloated stomach, those little sounds of digestion gurgling up and creating music in his eardrums.

The moon washes clean through broken windows, casting glints upon the nameless act that was carried out in this endless room. No stains, no blood. Montgomery tidied up.

It is a fine night in Ohio. A night for lovers and satiated appetites.

THE PEAR TREE

Lyca rides the rails and roams the streets, her boots held together with tape and twine, and when you have no home there's never a real destination. She sojourns in this city with the dead gutted buildings just because it's a place she woke up to while in the boxcar, and she looked out as the train slowed, the wind tousling through her blonde dreads, and she thought it would be as good as anywhere to ramble through for a while.

It isn't much of a city. It's a place where coal once thrived, but the mines have gone dry, and now it's just a valley of pain nestled into the Appalachians. The people are hollow-eyed, slaves to heroin, and there's no hope for them. She doesn't engage, and she doesn't bother. She's seen where that road leads. She's been there before, and filling up emptiness with false pleasure has never served her long-term. It only deepens the stain.

It's hard to remember exactly when she noticed the pear tree. It is where it does not belong. A little patch of scrubby grass between a row of brick apartments in a Section 8 ghetto across from a long-abandoned sock factory with broken windows and a sagging tar roof. No orchards or farms for many miles in either direction, so it's clear to Lyca that the tree is alone, and she wonders about its origin. Who planted the seed? What cruel twist of fate decided to put such a pretty growing thing in such a terrible place?

There's no one around, and it's late summer, so she decides she'll stay awhile. There's a little underpass not far from the brick apartments, and she'll create a nest for herself down there with a sleeping bag and the few meager belongings that are left to her. There's something about that pear tree. The roots have gotten to her soul, and she knows that she wants to paint it. Lyca sees something beyond the bark. The leaves want to speak, but there has never been anyone who cared enough to listen. So she'll stay awhile, she'll observe, and she'll paint.

It might be possible to capture something that has gone unseen. Lyca doesn't believe she has many talents. She's tried to participate society before, but it spat her out, and that implanted the idea in her head that it found her distasteful. So she dislodged, and she became a woman apart. She walks and watches, just existing, and a part of her knows that her purpose has darkened inside of her like a match that never had the proper fuel to become a blaze worth remembering.

But she likes to paint. She likes to observe and look as deeply into something or someone as she possibly can. The longer you watch, the more you open yourself up to the possibility of understanding. It's something most people don't care about, because they look for only the briefest moment, and if the subject doesn't immediately interest them, they look away forever. Lyca has always thought that's very unfair. Everything in this world deserves a second look and a longer consideration.

She sinks into the grass, finding a comfortable cross-legged position, and she searches her battered denim knapsack covered with band patches for her tools. She retrieves a fresh canvas and positions it on a little retractable metal stand, and next come her paints and her brushes, all the colors of the rainbow.

Her strange green eyes flit over the tree, and she drinks in the details, savoring the taste. The trunk is thick and generous, the roots deep enough to find nourishment. They travel as far as a cracked sidewalk several yards away, and they jut up from the shattered concrete like baby serpents seeking the sun. The leaves are lush, and they have a glow to them. The branches reach skyward with yearning optimism, and bumblebees flit through them, darting around and sucking up sweetness wherever sweetness is offered.

Lyca mixes yellow for the bees, green for the leaves, and brown for the trunk. She doesn't think much. She just acts, and she lets herself fall into those colors. She starts slow, and then she finds her groove. There's a pleasant hum in her head, and she doesn't know if it's the bees or if it originated from within her. It doesn't matter.

It's a good tree. It didn't ask to be here. It didn't choose the soil from which it grew. It's doing the best that it can, and Lyca tries her best to capture that. She blends and she shades and she works until the sun is low in the sky and the clouds turn gunmetal gray while floating above the branches. She lets her mind drift, and she imagines tiny hands extending from the branches, reaching up as high as they can possibly go. It's like the tree knows deep in its heartwood that this isn't where it's supposed to be. It's reaching for something, but with difficulty and that something seems out of its grasp.

It would be better if there were other pear trees around it. A nice orchard where companions are to the left and to the right, but that luxury is not afforded. The tree is alone, and it has no others to learn from. It must grow without guidance, and that can hurt a tree sometimes.

But the tree is trying, and that is the emphasis of Lyca's piece. She fades out the surroundings, making them indistinct.

The ugly brick buildings, the failed factories and rusted railways, the people slouching along like empty scarecrows. These are vague background details, and the tree is the centerpiece. It is life. It is growth.

She spends her summer painting the tree over and over again from a variety of different angles. Lyca finds that she's searching for something in each piece. She wants an answer to the question that has been hurting her inside for a very long time.

Can something special grow from a sad and forgotten place?

Lyca stays until autumn, and she works obsessively. She witnesses the ripening of fruit, the slow fattening of pears meant to be bitten into and savored. She paints it all, and she barely finds time to sleep or eat. It's a mania that has settled into her bones, and it isn't the first time. The curse of the artist. When she's feeling it, she knows that she mustn't stop until she captures on the canvas the magic that flirts with her.

No one can understand aside from a fellow creative. It's that internal itch that comes to artists and writers and those with the lamentable need to make something from nothing. It must be done, or it will consume you. It can't stay within. Lyca knows that if she doesn't vent the artistic urge, it will decay inside of her body and leave her immobile.

And speaking of decay, that is what she paints, because that is now the fate of the pear tree. The pears grow too plump to remain tethered to the branches, and they fall to the earth, plummeting back down against the soil which birthed them. They linger in the dirt, and they rot, sending up a pungent sickly sweetness into the air. This isn't how it's meant to be. Beautiful fruit is meant to be picked. If this were an orchard or a homestead or even the side yard of an elderly couple with a taste for pears, this wouldn't have happened. But the circumstances of the pear tree's environment have made this inevitable. There are no happy people to pluck the pears, to gather them, to make yummy recipes from them.

The pears fall, and the pears rot. The best they can hope for is a midnight nibble from a rabbit or to be consumed quickly by burrowing insects. Lyca feverishly paints the decomposition. The stinking browns and the dying yellows. The ruined softness of broken pear flesh, and plump pieces of fruit sinking into puddles that cannot mean anything to anyone.

There's a predominant emotion in her work, and it is anger. The anger stems from the wasted potential of the pear tree. Elsewhere it could have been a bountiful gift, and it could have been appreciated. The pears wouldn't bake in the sun, effectively made worthless.

She slashes her brush across canvas after canvas, making a knife of it, painting the dying and the decay of something that could have been so much more. Lyca doesn't fully understand why this affects her so much, but it does. She thinks that she sees something in the tree that she sees in herself. Wasted potential. Gifts that birth maggots instead of success. The air is bitter in her nostrils, soft sour fruit, and she uses the bitterness to her advantage. She lets the bitterness overtake her, and she paints like something is clawing from beneath her breasts with the intention to break free.

She lets herself feel what she feels. She feels hateful, bitter, and infuriated. How did it get this bad? How does a hole form around you before you even notice that it was ever there at all?

She wants to blame someone, to transfer the anguish, but there is no one to take it. She only has herself, so she gives it to herself. Lyca thrusts her brush into the dead flesh of the pears, smearing it around in that mess, and she paints with the literal rot. Lost inside her own head, lost in the rotting fruit, lost in the bitter branches of the pear tree.

At some point it begins to rain, her dreads become plastered across her haunted face, and she barely notices when night comes and all light dies. The pear tree contorts on the canvas, becoming disfigured, something that craves nonexistence simply to lessen the pain of life. The pain of circumstances. The toll of being born to an environment that poisons you instead of nurtures you.

Lyca is soaked when she gathers her paintings to her chest and stumbles off to her sleeping bag beneath the underpass. She is exhausted and her body immediately succumbs, a shivering slumber that still thrums with the creative fever that overtook her.

She's thinking even as she sleeps.

The thinking never stops.

She awakens to the sky cracking open like a bottle across her forehead, a blaze of blue painting the darkness in unnatural light. The night smells of smoke, and she sees tiny red embers floating in the breeze near the mouth of the underpass.

She fights her way out of the sleeping bag and climbs the hill, and she sees the pear tree there, lit up bright to rival the streetlamps. Her muse is burning, the lightning bolt that struck it having left a deep blackened scar in the upper portion of the trunk. There's a beauty in the burning, and it makes Lyca's heart ache to see it. She digs into her pockets, pulling out a wrinkled piece of sketch paper and a nub of charcoal, and she thinks that it must still be raining, because droplets are hitting the paper as she holds it up. But the rain has stopped, and she realizes that she's weeping, and her tears stain the paper.

She draws as fast as she can, scratching out the tree as it exists in its final moments. That vibrant conflagration, merciful flames, and the consumption of something that grew even when it shouldn't have. The smell of rot is gone, replaced by an aromatic scent of fruit baked to a pleasant temperature in the oven.

Lyca lets herself feel what she feels. Sorrow, grief, and a deep sense of release. She feels like she's watching herself burning. A part of her that no longer serves her. A lost little girl trapped in a bad place with bad thoughts and a future that rotted before it ever had the opportunity to ripen.

She doesn't see death in those flames. She sees a remaking and a reshaping. A cleansing that came late, but at least it came.

Her fingers are black with charcoal, and she kneels and reaches out, rubbing them into the ash that drifts down from the withering branches.

She rubs the last of the pear tree into the canvas with her bare fingertips, and she deepens the roots.

There's not much left in the morning. Just a brittle charred stump where a pear tree used to be. Lyca has packed up her possessions, and her knapsack is firmly affixed to her back, bulging with paintings and sketches that threaten to spill over.

She goes to the stump, and she reaches out her hand, rubbing against the remnants of the trunk. It's warm to the touch, and when she makes contact, she wants to believe that a message enters her mind.

Thank you for seeing me instead of my circumstances.

Thank you for understanding that I tried.

Her fingers want to linger because the warmth feels good, but she knows it cannot last. It's time to move on from this bad place, and it's time to grow. She starts to turn away, and then she notices that a few feet away on the ground, a single pear survived the fire.

She bends down to pick it up, and she brushes off the cinders and burnt twigs. It's ripe and flawless, the skin glowing, and Lyca thinks to herself that she has never in her life seen a more perfect pear. A piece of fruit befitting the Garden of Eden instead of a scrubby patch of grass in a town that long ago breathed its last.

She does what anyone else would do when presented with such a treat. She bites into the pear, and she relishes the sweetness on her tongue. It's juicy and it's good and it is exactly what it is supposed to be.

She stands there eating the pear until it is all gone, and she tosses the remnants behind her and licks her fingers clean. Her tongue rolls against her teeth, and she finds the special thing that is worth saving.

She spits a glossy black seed into her palm, and she rubs a thumb against it, liking the texture. There's so much possibility in that little black object, and that thought alone makes her smile.

Lyca lovingly tucks the seed into her pocket, and she heads off to find a better place.

When she does find it, she thinks that the first thing she'll do is plant a little pear tree.

 SIREN SONG

The father drives, hands tight on the steering wheel, and he contemplates his family in the rearview mirror with a flat gaze of resentment. His son in the backseat of the SUV, chin smeared in strawberry ice cream, voice a shrill drone, sticky fingers smacking up against the window and delighting at the annoying thud that follows each time. His teenage daughter chewing gum, a vapid automaton, consumed by her smartphone and her garish jewelry and how many likes and comments she gets on her TikTok videos.

And then there is the mother, the wife, the bane of his existence, sunburned cheeks and chest, freckled nose, manicured nails, and those withering eyes that seem to take great pleasure in making him feel inferior as a husband. This is his life. This is his family. He is not happy, and he feels trapped by these entities that depend on him and expect things of him. There's a secret loathing in his heart that he does not give voice to, and he wonders if other men with families feel the same. Do they like their children? Do they actually love their wives?

He wonders . . .

The drive has been brutal, and it isn't the normal summer vacation for them. Usually they'd pile into the car and go to some commercialized local beach like Ocean City, Maryland, where diapers float along the shore, humans are packed together like simmering sardines, and the boardwalk is a perfect advertisement for how horrendously overpopulated this planet is. But not this year. This year his wife crowed and nagged and hounded him, and she demanded something new and exotic. He acquiesced as he often does just to keep the peace, and he found an Airbnb listing to suit their purposes. A small cottage along a private tropical beach in a sparsely populated part of Florida, only accessible through a winding road passing through a wetland. Henshaw's Roost, it's called, and the photographs managed to impress the father. White beaches, sand like tumbled sugar, the Atlantic a turquoise balm to soothe the anxious skin of a burdened man.

They're driving through the wetland now, and the wildlife is out in abundance. Cranes watch them pass, crooked necks twisting to monitor their progress. The father has driven over two serpents already, not bothering to stop, relishing the thump of their segmented bodies bursting under the tires. He was forced to stop when a large mother alligator ran across the road, side-eyeing them with prehistoric indifference. She looked at him like he had no business being there. The father didn't care for that. He's a proud man who demands respect from all lesser things, his family included.

This swampland vista seems to stretch on forever, and he hopes that it will end soon. He's ready to reach their destination so that he can crack into the bourbon that he brought along, settle himself on the beach, and let the sun blister away his discontentment. He's tired of screaming kids and conversations with the wife that loop and go nowhere. If it wasn't such a societal taboo, he would slap the faces of his children until those loose lips learned to seal. He would take his wife by the throat, and he would throttle her, thumbs deep in the wattles of her neck, shaking and bashing her against the windshield until she learned to leave him alone for just a millisecond.

Is that too much to ask? It is too much for a man to crave a bit of serenity just for himself?

Maybe he's selfish. He leans over the steering wheel and he broods. His wife complains that the AC isn't putting out enough air. His son digs little fingers up into little nostrils, searching for snot to pull out onto his little shirt. His daughter sighs and rolls her eyes and chews that *fucking* bubble gum like a cow that thinks she's too good for the slaughterhouse. It's not fair for him to be saddled with these demons. These soul-sucking creatures that share his blood but seem oblivious to his thoughts and his feelings . . .

He thinks of all the news stories he's seen about *family annihilators*. Those poor haunted men who are pushed so far that they bludgeon their own into lifeless carcasses. Sometimes he envies their bravery, their willingness to cut the cord for ultimate peace. Surely such cases are not the fault of those long-suffering husbands and fathers. They were driven to it, compelled to do it, and he sympathizes with them. But he can't do it. Too much scrutiny, too much blowback, and he fears the repercussions . . .

He must endure these contemptible pieces of human baggage until he's old and gray, and then maybe when he's dead, it'll be quiet. So he grits his teeth, he creases his brow, and he forces a smile for his wife. It's a family vacation. Memories for the photo album. The best years of his life, right?

Ever since he drove into the wetland, he's been hearing a soft and reassuring voice in the center of his head. He's not sure where it's coming from, but he likes it. Sounds like reeds rubbing together, shells tumbling in the tide, and a note of submissive feminine yearning.

It tells him that the sea will understand. The sea will accept that he was never meant for this, and it will usher him past the mediocrity that shackles him. He'll be a king with a crown of conch, and he'll feast on the most succulent fish and be pampered under palm trees. There's hope in the lapping waves. Something nests in the dying coral beyond Henshaw's Roost, and that something wants the best for him. He deserves that.

He sees pale cerulean eyes and parted lips in his mind.

He daydreams of the tasting of them, salty and tart, big calloused hand planted firmly on a lower back moist with brine. She's waiting. She's his liberation.

The mother exits the vehicle, and she appraises the cottage on the hill. The wind from the ocean is warm, and it teases her floppy hat and caresses the curves beneath her sundress. She takes a few steps forward, appreciating the white sand beneath her sandals. Her husband is a man who does many things wrong, but maybe he did something right for once in choosing this place for their vacation. She spares him a glance, and her stomach feels unsettled at the sight of him. Graying temples, gut hanging over his belt, glasses smudged with thumbprints. When was the last time she felt attracted to this man? When was the last time she felt anything at all for him other than a mild undercurrent of revulsion?

She was a vision in her prime, gorgeous to the point of having multiple suitors just hoping for a chance, but then she chose, and it was like a slow downward spiral. She's middle-aged now; it seems like whole chapters from the book that was meant to be her life got torn out and rewritten without her consent. Unplanned pregnancies and the ravages to her body, and no matter how hard she exercised, those scars and folds and excess pounds always seemed reluctant to depart. She could have married so many different men. Men that went on to become lawyers, doctors, and millionaires. But she settled on a dud. She picked the runt of the biological litter, and her choice has long embittered her. An average wage, an average face, and he has nothing to offer her but an average life . . .

They're exploring the cottage now, her sandals held in her hand, and it's a cozy little place. Tiny living room, lofts, and a patio with a view of the shore. Her son runs in circles through each room, bellowing like a dinosaur, and she often wonders if there is something wrong with him. His mind seems dim like a bulb on the verge of burning out. She once caught him out in the backyard with a butter knife from the kitchen, and he was sitting there in the mud, using the dull blade to cut into the bloated bodies of banana slugs. His hands were smeared in their guts and their foul mucus, and he lifted up his palms and showed them to her, tittering like it was the funniest thing in the universe.

A smelly, sticky, and often unreachable child, and the few times she held him in her arms after his birth, it was like trying to mother a dull lump of paste. She never wanted him. She needs only to run her fingertips over the tiger-stripe stretch marks on her lower abdomen to remind her just how much she wishes that he had never slid out of her.

And then there is her daughter. That haughty, preening narcissist. Addicted to social media and seemingly soulless. The mother remembers feeling joy when she found out that she'd be having a girl, but it crumbled to dust when the child grew and never developed a personality. Instead, there is just a void to fill up with things. Clothes, trinkets, gadgets. She can't remember the last time she and her daughter had a genuine conversation. Every clipped sentence is a joust, a struggle for power and control.

What has she done to earn such a loveless existence? Why did God saddle her with broken children and a bore of a husband? Will it ever get better, or is this just the sickening weight of her present and her future?

She floats into the bathroom, hand reaching out to flip the light switch on. There's a modest shower, a porcelain tub, and a mirror with unforgiving illumination. It shines on all of her flaws and the pockmarked bits of herself that she tries to slather away with makeup. Moles, skin dents, and the cruel sagging of age.

She listens to the stomping of her son's feet in the cottage, the asthmatic breathing of her dullard husband, and the infernal finger-clacking of her daughter texting and messaging and posting to Twitter. It would be so easy to crush her forehead into that mirror, shatter it, and jam a shard of glass into her own jugular. That would show them. This ungrateful, unfulfilling family of hers would learn to appreciate her then.

She's actually considering it, weighing the pros and cons and how much blood will splash out into the sink and how badly it'll hurt, but she gets distracted. She finds herself drawn to the large bay windows on one side of the cottage, the light silk curtains drawn aside to present a view of the ocean.

The sun is dipping on the horizon, and all is painted in reds and golds, and something about the sight of the sunset stirs the romanticism that hibernates inside of her. She keeps thinking that she hears a voice. It's deep, masculine, and it makes her feel safe. The voice is full of promises, and the mother finds that it comforts her. It tells of waters that restore youth, the security and grandeur of palaces in the deep, and beautiful iridescent children that smile and behave and swim happily around her ankles.

It's a voice just for her, and she takes pains to hide it from her family. She doesn't want them to hear it. Maybe it's a fantasy, but it's *her* fantasy. She places her hand upon the window, pressing her palm to the glass, and it feels cool against her skin. The ocean seems so old out there. So terribly, eternally old.

And if the voice speaks truly, it has secrets to show her.

The son whoops and hollers and leaps, running across the beach, stumpy legs carrying him along as he reaches in the direction of the sky, wishing he could stretch his arms and pull the squawking gulls down into his fists. He'd open them with his fingers, scrub his face in the red that drips out, and then he'd break their nice yellow beaks and snap off their brittle legs just to hear the sound it makes.

He likes when things show the red that is within. It is fun to hurt things, but he doesn't like to be hurt. Sometimes his father yells when he does things like that. His father is ugly, and he hates him. If the son wasn't so small, he'd take his colored pencil and stick it into his father's face until it was all red, the ugliness covered up with a nice wet mask. It's different with his mother. He likes to scare her and make her face twist into funny expressions. It's fun to show her his hobbies and experiments. She always gives him long talks about how what he's doing isn't nice and those animals and bugs feel things just like he feels things.

But the son knows that they feel things. He does things to them because he knows that they feel. He wants them to feel. It is better to pull something apart when it is feeling and screaming. Maybe when he grows bigger he will pull apart his sister and make her play with him.

He begins to explore, walking along the beach and picking up shells and looking into tiny holes where crabs might live. His mother and father are setting up a big umbrella and laying out towels. His sister is spraying sunscreen on and looking at her bikini in the selfie camera on her phone. They barely notice him, and that makes him so mad. They never have time to be excited about the things that he gets excited about. Maybe when they are sleeping tonight he will pee on their toothbrushes and then not tell them, so in the morning they'll learn a lesson. He thinks about lots of games like that when he's coloring. His parents don't seem to like his pictures, because they never put them on the refrigerator at home.

The son loves to draw swirls with black crayon, big jagged loops over and over again, and then a little red face in the middle with a frown. He gives the pictures to his mother and his father, and he hopes that the pictures will make them frown. It usually works.

He wanders farther away from them, and sunset makes his eyeballs hurt. It's blinding him, and he wishes he could rip it down and squash it into the sand. He's usually angry, but he's been learning how to hide that inside of himself. He keeps it there in his heart as a treat for when he's in a particular mood. When he does let it out, he wants it to be big and booming and messy.

It's weird, but the son thinks that he hears something out in the ocean whispering to him. At first he thought it was just the gulls, but this sound is beneath the constant din of the shrieking seabirds. He can't tell if it's a man or woman, because it sounds like both. It talks to him the way he wants to be talked to. It talks like the mommy and daddy he wishes that he had, so different from the ones he's stuck with.

The voice says it will give him things to play with. Sharp things, heavy things, and weak things that he can stab and hit until he's tired and ready for bed. It says he is a promised prince and he can wear a cape of seaweed and he will be able to fly over the dark chasms down below. He won't have any rules, and no one will tell him what to do. He'll be his own captain, and he can steer the sunken ghost ships and have all the lost treasure chests that he wants.

He won't have to wear normal clothes if he goes down there. He will get an eyepatch and a wooden leg, and a white shirt that billows. He can wear a big black hat so that everyone will know that they have to listen to him.

And if anyone doesn't listen, he can take his sharp pirate sword, and he can slide it into their bellies. He can cut them up and look at what comes out. And he won't be punished for it, because it's normal in the depths. It's very black and no sunshine can get down there, so no one will be able to see the things that he does. He likes that a lot. It means he can do things that he has only ever dreamed of doing.

The boy stands on the beach and tugs at his swimming trunks, his vacant black eyes staring out into the water. The sun is starting to go away completely, and his lousy parents won't want to stay out much longer. But he'd like to stay longer.

He likes the night. It's easier to do things at night when everything is quiet and empty and no one notices. The voice says that it's always night where it is. Night is home. He is already thinking about what he has to do to get down there. He is good at making plans and not telling anyone about his plans.

The son spots a crab scuttling along, and he crouches down next to it. It looks up at him, claws twitching, eyes just little black droplets. He puts his grimy fingers onto the crab's stalk eyes, and he squeezes them until they burst, making his hands warm and gooey. And then he lets it live without eyes. It will be worse for it if it lives, and the son wants that for it.

He doesn't want the crab to see his secrets. He doesn't want anyone to see and tell on him. The thing that whispers from the sea is a secret worth keeping.

The daughter lounges in a hammock on the shoreline, her sun-kissed skin feeling cool now that the daylight has faded and the moon has come out to play. She shakes her bare foot from side to side, her ankle bracelet making music, and she's lost in the screen of her phone. It's a competition for her, and if she doesn't stay on top of things, she'll backslide and get less likes and comments on her content. She's already been distracted by her family for the majority of this trip. In a perfect world she'd be able to just shut them up with a click of a button, muting them like the messages she receives in her DMs when she's not in the mood to reply.

Her father who drones on about nothing, her mother who always wants to argue, and her creepy little brother who likes to sit around and eat worms. She feels like a different species than them. She's actually hot, and they're just the most digital feet and open up wide to be fed whatever trend or fad she wants them to digest. Pathetic individuals. She can't wait for the day when she moves out and gains her independence, because it won't be hard for her to cut ties and move on to bigger and better things. She knows that she's meant for big cities, glamorous traveling, and a life befitting someone like her. She's a social media influencer, so she deserves that. And the best her father could do was this little slice of nothing in Florida? What a dud of a vacation . . .

The daughter heaves a sigh and checks her apps again, making sure that engagement remains high. She finds that she often burns with envy when she sees other girls in her social circle getting more attention than her. Why should her selfie get only five-thousand likes when a girl who isn't even half as pretty as her manages to pass the ten-thousand threshold? It wouldn't hurt to think of a rumor or something to sabotage her competition. It's a cutthroat game, but the daughter believes that it's better to strike first before they can do it to you.

She's always had quite the creative streak when it comes to orchestrating the downfall of others. A little smile tugs at the corner of her mouth, and she reaches up to fix her lip gloss. It's actually peaceful out here at night, the moonbeams like butter on her skin, and the sound of the tide lapping in and out makes her feel like taking a power nap. Her family settled into the cottage, but she wanted to gain some separation from them before going to bed, and the hammock seemed like the ideal spot for it.

Her eyes fall across the ocean, and it appears as an immense dark animal, breathing and rippling, so much eldritch strength in those roaring waves. There's something far out, close to the horizon. It's a small black speck, and what the hell could that be? Driftwood, garbage, or maybe even a little boat?

The daughter sits up on the hammock and squints, but the moon only provides so much illumination, and it isn't immediately clear what she's looking at until the shape starts to glide closer. At first she thinks it's a seal or an otter, but the outline appears vaguely human, or at least something approximating a human shape. It's visible from the torso up, skin the color of oil, so inky that it blends into the dark water, and onyx curls flow down around its shoulders. It appears feminine, and it just floats there far beyond the beach, watching the daughter. It has huge eyes, blazing orange, and they remind the girl of lanterns hanging from the porch of an old manor house.

The daughter isn't sure how to react until the whispers start. They travel across a massive distance, but they're still strong enough to pierce her ears. Her anxiety immediately melts away, and she finds that looking into those burning orange orbs gives her a sense of belonging.

It tells of fame, fortune, and a life of purpose. It tells of worship under the sea. It speaks of forgotten fathoms where she will have no competition because she'll be the only goddess present. Servants to fawn over her, lovers to beg for her affection. A life of leisure, and the daughter practically swoons at the thought . . .

The shape is beckoning to her, hands with long fingers, a lavender webbing between each digit. The whispers all jumble together, and soon it becomes a song. Melodies of promise, lyrics of temptation, and the angelic voice is a like a harpsichord that speaks the language of the heart. It is a ballad that rises and falls for the sake of avarice, and the daughter finds that she's walking across the beach in the direction of the shape. She barely feels the sand beneath her feet, and the moonbeams are dazzling her, leaving her in a state of intoxication.

She has to get closer. She wants to hear more of this nightsong. Her legs carry her out into the water, and she wades freely into the ocean. The water is incredibly cold, but the song is warm, so it doesn't matter. Her heels crush down on broken shells, and seaweed catches along her wrists as she pumps her way forward. She doesn't think to swim. The idea of swimming is the farthest thing from her mind, and so she walks, and at some point, her head dunks down beneath the water, a few gurgling bubbles coming up to mark her passage. Her lungs fill with salt, and still she walks. The light of the cottage becomes nothing but a pinprick, but she keeps trudging across the bottom of the ocean.

Something is coming to embrace her.

Something with big lantern eyes and a mouth full of hollow needle teeth. It sings as it comes for her.

All sirens must sing for their supper.

The siren strips the flesh and picks the bones, and then she carries the daughter's wayward soul down to the sunken island of Anthemusa, her flowery necropolis. It's a habitat for those lost spirits that are forever doomed to flit through shipwrecks and labyrinthine coral, and it pleases the siren to have the company of those she has fed upon.

It is a full night for her, so she doesn't linger after dropping off her new arrival. She returns to the edge of the shore, her brittle wet wings twitching along her upper back, and she calls out to the others in song. Each individual requires a song tailored to their fantasies, much like a fisherman procuring the proper lure for each unique catch.

The father stumbles from the cottage first, taking pains not to wake his wife sleeping next to him. He stinks of sour dreams and a half-mast erection, and he wades into the sea like a zombie, arms reaching out to take hold of her. She meets his embrace with talons like razors, and when the blood pools from him, she has to act fast to keep the sharks from scavenging what belongs to her by right. His confused soul is dropped into her den, and then hours later she's back at it, her music taking on a deep masculine note.

The mother comes holding daintily to her nightgown, hoping for a tryst with a midnight caller, and she sees what she is compelled to see. To her, the siren is tall and dark, with wide shoulders, grizzled cheeks, and orange eyes that radiate protection. The mother awkwardly flops out into the sea, showing the siren her cheek and hoping for a soft kiss, and instead that cheek is bitten down to the sinew. The spirit is harvested, and the flesh is consumed.

The little boy is saved for last. He is strange, and he requires a strange song. The siren sings of bloodshed, torment, and pain he can inflict with impunity. He doggie-paddles out to her, half-drowned by the time he's within reach, and his breath is like curdled milk in her nostril slits. She teaches him pain, and he learns the sound of his own screams. He makes his own song, and it is his last.

She pirouettes into the depths and acts as a stork, casting the vile babe down onto her floral island with the rest of his kin. It's a silent sanctuary, a collection of souls, and sailors from generations past lie on beds of algae, their mouths sending up whispered prayers that always go unanswered.

The siren has hunted more than she needs tonight, so she thinks it best to rest. She curls up into the fetal position, drawing blankets of kelp around her scrawny shoulders, and she watches the seahorses peck at her eyelashes.

The family has amassed into one group, their souls bound even in this deathlessness. The father starts to bellow. The mother starts to needle him with verbal barbs. The son begins to giggle like a maniac, and the daughter admonishes him with the shrill voice of a harpy. A conflict among damned souls, and the bickering builds up to a crescendo. It is a bad song, an ugly song, and the siren does not like it. She tries to cover her ears with her hands, but that doesn't work. She drags kelp over her head and pushes it down like a pillow, but she cannot drown them out. They're crowing at each other, a hateful spew of words without thought, and she would like to shred their flesh to shut them up, but there is no flesh left to defile. There is nothing she can do to quiet them, and that realization hits her like a hammerhead to the abdomen.

The family is desecrating the perfect stillness of her den. There is a corruption in them, and the souls are spoiled, spiritual meat that is sure to sicken. They get louder and louder, and their song wilts her flowers, scares her seahorses, and unsettles even the catatonic spirits that have been with her for centuries.

She bursts up from her bedding and twirls in a circle, clamping her talons across her ears, and she tries to comfort herself with her own music, but it's just a little harmonica in comparison to the boiling cacophony that is coming out of these people. They shout and rage and prick at each other, and the toxicity is pulling apart her nest, causing ships to topple, rusted anchors to rattle, and bubbles of unclean air to float into her gills and explode inside of her.

She wants to flutter to them and beg them to stop, beg them for peace, but it's pointless. This is a broken family, and everyone around them must endure the shards of that break. It whittles her down, and she feels small.

The siren falls to the ocean floor and begins to crawl, webbed fingers digging for purchase. The family's flesh churns in her stomach, and it doesn't feel right. It's poison, and how did she manage to overlook that? This hunt is her undoing, this family her karma.

She starts to sing again, and her throat feels raw. She sings to bury the hopelessness and the anxiety and the fear. She is a child looking up at big adult shapes that are shouting and hurting each other, oblivious to the damage it is doing to her. The long-term damage. Trauma like a seed that knows only how to spread deep roots, and she doesn't envy that gardener that tries to prune it back.

The song is shriveling in her throat, becoming lost inside of her, and for the first time in a thousand years, she is voiceless. No one hears her. No one cares to hear.

Consuming the family was a grave mistake.

I f you call from the dusty streets of southern Gullytown, up on Darksome Hill, there sits a rider on a dead horse, and his name is Scorpion Bill. You'll smell him when he comes, because his horse is sun-baked and rotten, and worms breed in its flaring nostrils. He's a void beneath his hat, the rim a great concealment, and his coat is pinkened leather, lathered in new blood that stains like raspberries fresh from the bush. There's rust on his revolvers, and when the bullets fly, they tend to split off into little fragments of shrapnel.

Scorpion Bill favors a gutshot, because it's slow, and he believes in the power of savoring things. He's been known to crouch down next to a man that's been gifted with his lead, bleeding there in the dirt, the saloon mere yards away, and he'll take his long pale spider-fingers and gather up a bit of gravel before pushing it down into those abdominal holes, mixing chewed-up red gut ropes with rock and soil and pieces of earth sure to be infectious.

The man will stare up at Scorpion Bill while moaning for mother, eyes rolling in the head like a wounded elk, and that old saddle-sore will give him a grin as he rubs the pain in deeper. Bill's grin is a desert, for it is barren of emotion, and if you look close enough, you can see the tumbleweeds and the bleached coyote bones that live behind his teeth.

No one knows what Scorpion Bill is. He ain't a man. He ain't born of blood and meat like you or me. He behaves like no ghost I ever heard tell of. I don't think he's the walking dead, and I don't know if he's a devil or not. This is hard country, and devils are everywhere, so it's difficult to tell. It makes no sense that he keeps that horse walking when it's fit for the grave. He doesn't hunt for bounties, and he's not at war with the law. He's no savior when it comes to brigands, and he's one of the few individuals seen around Gullytown that never frequents the whorehouse. His needs lean sanguinary, and he satisfies them somewhere far from the inner thighs of a woman.

Sometimes he comes down from Darksome Hill, never at a time that can be predicted, and he'll make mischief where there was none before. He'll talk at you if you let him, and he only has the worst things to say. Places he's been that are sour, ugly deeds he's seen done in his time, and personal things that he has no right to know. We've all seen him rambling in the hours of shimmering sun when the heat is so bad it threatens to boil you and melt your spurs, and it's best to look down at your own shoes when he comes riding. Few see his face, but I imagine it's like blistered hardpan, because that's what we cast our eyes upon whenever he's about.

His pockets are always moving. You'll see them twitching and bulging, because he keeps things in those pockets. Critters and vermin and small angry animals from the badlands. He has a favorite species of pet, and I guess that's how he got his name. If you make the mistake of looking at him for too long, he'll reach deep into the pockets of that plasma-pink duster, and he'll show you handfuls of scorpions that skitter lovingly on his palms.

I've been unlucky enough to see what he likes to do with those scorpions. I'll tell you, but lean in close, and don't steal my pipe tobacco, because I know how much of it I got left.

He walks into town, and he finds someone that he wants to play with. That poor soul will do anything and everything to get away from him. I've seen them run, hide, and try their damndest to fight him off. If they run, he rides them down. If they hide, he whistles for them, and he always knows exactly where they are. But it's fighting him that's the biggest mistake of them all. If you fight Scorpion Bill, he resents that you think you have a chance in hell to come out of it alive. He takes that personally.

He beats on you first, closed fists, and his knuckles feel like oxen hooves kicking at full strength. It doesn't take long for a fella to go down, and then he's on you, and that's where he thrives. Those scorpions come crawling from his sleeves, and they're loyal to their master, and he has always had a way with them.

It hurts like hell to take a sting from a scorpion to an arm or a leg, but it's bearable. It'll throb for a while, and then after a couple of hours, if you ice it well and take care, the bump will go down and you'll be alright. But that ain't how he guides that stinger. He'll straddle a fella, and he'll pinch that scorpion's tail, and he'll drive the barbed needle of that stinger directly into the jelly of an eyeball. He'll do it again and again, pumping that hot caustic venom into a man's sensitive peepers, and if one scorpion gets tired and stops stinging, it gets tossed over the shoulder and a substitute takes its place.

As I said before, Scorpion Bill don't rush. He takes his time with the stinging. You know what happens to a man's eyeballs when they've been pumped full of stinger juice a hundred or so times? I'll tell you, but you'll wish I hadn't.

Those jellies swell up almost as big as wagon wheels, pushing soft and meaty from the eyelids, vessels all burst and bleeding, and the man is blinded forever. He cries rivers of pain, leaking out that venom, and Scorpion Bill likes to let him up to stagger around and reach for anyone or anything that might deliver him from his fate.

That should be the end of it, but it ain't never the end. Scorpion Bill will let the blind bastard shamble for a bit until he's had a considerable chuckle before he kicks his legs out from under him, and he pulls his trousers down to his ankles in front of the whole town. You have to understand that no one tries to stop Scorpion Bill. No one interferes. People just stand and watch, because they don't know what the hell else they can do.

He likes to humiliate just as much as he hurts. So ol' Bill strips that man of his britches, his cock a scared shriveled worm in the dust, and he leans down and twists up on that scrotum, making sure the balls are taut in his hand, and then he lets the scorpions come again, and he makes them sting those testicles as many times as they stung the eyes.

It's the same fate, just a different part of the anatomy. The testicles become enormous, huge swollen cannonballs that drag on the hardpan, leaking that venom juice, and the scrotum becomes so stretched from the process that it often tears. Scorpion Bill stands up tall after that, towering with his duster blowing in the acrid wind, and he lets the fella rise up and shamble around again.

Blind with full jellied eyes and balls scraping in the dirt as he hobbles for some haven that never comes. It's like seeing a disfigured jester, a man turned into a mewling monkey, and Scorpion Bill pulls from his holster a heavy gun that catches the sunbeams, and he aims, and his aim is always true.

He puts bullets into the eyes, and they splash out, clear venom popping from deflated balloons, and it's the same with the balls, bullets singing as they pierce and pop those distended sexual organs. The poison bursts out in a torrent, and the breeze often catches it, and sometimes it splashes in the faces of watching children, burning their faces and making them bury their noses against a mother's skirt.

That's the kind of mischief that Scorpion Bill likes best.

That's how he gets his rocks off, and once he's done, he'll talk at folks for a while, and then he'll ride back to whatever den he has up there on Darksome Hill.

I remember watching him that one summer evening with sweat pouring down from my temples, and before he climbed back on that dead horse, he looked at me, and he said some words.

I can't recall if it was a mouth or a set of mandibles that he spoke to me with, but I do recall the words.

"You'll meet a woman in ten years, and there will be love, and there will be marriage. You'll fill her belly with seed, and a baby will be born soon after. I'll come see you then."

I remember he spat in the dirt, and I thought it was tobacco, but I realized it wasn't when I saw the ground burned where he spat.

"When that baby is still daisy-fresh and only a few days out from the womb, I'm gonna drop it in this dirt, and I'm gonna stomp on its head until its blood and brains leak out like a busted tin can of tomato soup. I'll do it because it's somethin' to do."

I was gasping at him, wanting to do something to shut that hellhole gob, but I couldn't think of a single thing to say. I just stood there and took it, my legs wobbling, and I wanted to be anyone other than myself at that moment.

"I'll do it because when the day comes, I wanna see what you'll do. I wanna see what kind of a man it will make of you."

He wasted no more breaths, and he swept that duster out and climbed atop his horse that stunk of ruined meat, and then he was gone, just a galloping blur somewhere in the distance.

I've thought about him a lot since then. He's come and gone, but never again has he set his gaze on me. I hope he's forgotten, because his revelries are numerous, and I think it's easy to lose track.

But I'll tell ya, it worries me, because here soon, it's coming up on just about ten years.

did meet a woman. I did get married. I had me a baby girl, and I named her Belle, and she's just as plump and happy as they come. My wife is Grace, pure of heart and raised on a ranch out beyond Gullytown, and she loves that babe more than anything.

I was sweeping up the wooden slats in front of my barbershop when Scorpion Bill came riding, hat low, duster dripping red, and he lifted up those big hands and started counting on his fingers. He counted every calloused fingertip, and he stopped at ten.

"Been that long, Bill?"

The fear ate me up like a bear, but I didn't show it to him. I got the feeling he would have ate it up too.

"Just about."

Grace was rocking Belle in the shop chair, and she came out to see me, worried about the rider. She'd lived out on that isolated ranch all her days, so she hadn't ever had the pleasure of seeing Scorpion Bill face to face.

"I'll be having that lil' one."

"If you put a boot on my baby's head, you'll lose the foot in that boot, Bill."

I surprised myself saying that, but when my eyes fell on that sweet child that came from the woman I love, I knew I'd die or kill to protect her.

Scorpion Bill dismounted, and he came for me, and I pulled from my belt a straight razor and a leather strop. I held them tight in each hand, and when he bore down on me, I whipped that strop into his merciless face until my wrist ached, and I flicked open that razor and I cut him up so bad that he was bleeding from a thousand wounds, but it did no good, and he beat me nearly to death with his fists, and he cast me down to snuffle the dirt.

He pawed that babe from the clutches of my wife, and he planted Belle shrieking on the hardpan. He lifted a boot, his spur jangling, and he pressed his heel down tight against Belle's little baby head. He didn't put the pressure on too quick, because, like I've repeated, Scorpion Bill never liked making things fast. He wanted to crack that infant skull like a bird egg, and he wanted to take his sweet time doin' it.

He was inches away from squishing my newborn's brains out of her ears, and he would have done it, but a roaring banshee came up behind him. Grace had a big pair of long barber shears in her hands, and she yanked his pants down, and she cut his big gray dick off in one violent snip. It poured red like a hose, and she just went right on snipping, cutting off his ears, his nose, and ten fingers too. She tore the blades of those scissors up into his lower belly and she reached in with her fists and pulled out red ropes, making spools of them and tripping up his feet. She snipped more parts of Scorpion Bill off than I care to mention, and he never once did scream. At some point, the scorpions all fled from his duster, seeming to realize in their little arachnid brains that the master had fallen and a new home needed to be found.

He went down in the dirt next to me, breathing heavy, and I saw my wife drive those shears into his head until he didn't have a face no more, and then that was that.

She picked up her baby, and Belle was fine, just scared, but Grace cooed her all better. I loved my bloody bride more than ever at that moment.

I don't know what Scorpion Bill was. Maybe some devil, or a tired soothsayer, or just a sadist living up there on Darksome Hill. His horse didn't look so dead anymore. Just sickly, stinky, and coated in mange. It ran off after that, and no one ever saw it again.

See, here's the thing about Scorpion Bill. His legend preceded him. He was larger than life, and more than mortal to us. But my Grace never lived in Gullytown, and she never knew nothin' of his legend. Where fear froze us, she never hesitated. Her baby was in danger, and so she took those scissors, and she opened that rider up until she splattered all that he was onto the ground.

Sometimes perception ain't reality. We made a bogeyman of Bill in our minds, so that's what he became. But in the end, whatever kind of thing he was, he bled out, and he died. That's all there is left to say about the son of a bitch.

My wife looked real pretty even with her face all dripping scarlet. I think my baby will grow up to be like her. There's good land that's vacated now up on Darksome Hill, and soon, I'll build my family a house up there.

THE GIANT SEQUOIA

Bartholomew Stone—*Bart the Bastard* to his detractors, of which there were many—brought his traveling sideshow to the wild country of the western Sierra Nevada Mountains purely by reason of obsession. A long, slow trek to the coastal edges of California, all in pursuit of a great towering prize that a drifter told him about once during a backroom game of blackjack. It sparked something in Bart's ragged old heart, and he went to bed that night hearing coins jingling together, falling forever into his open palms.

He remembered the rasp of that drifter's voice, the way his words had whistled out through splintered wooden teeth.

"Nothin' like em' in all the world, I tell ya. These ain't just trees. These are fuckin' leviathans growing up outta the soil. You come upon them in the right light, and they blot out the sun, the moon, and the stars."

He'd leaned forward, and Bart could smell him, sweat like fetid onions, and a touch of gangrene from that oozing knife wound beneath his armpit that he'd bandaged haphazardly. He wouldn't tell how he came by the wound, and Bart hadn't given much of a damn either way.

"You want a marvel, Bart? Something the rubes will never forget? Go as far west as west goes, in those craggy hills close to the sea, and get yourself a giant sequoia. It'll take all the men you can gather to chop through her, but she'll be worth it. She'll make you a rich ol' saddle-sore, because trees like her don't exist nowhere else, and jaws will gape and pockets will empty at yer feet, of that you can be assured . . ."

A cunning wretch, that man was. Bart ended up having his own hired men kick the man's ribs in behind the main canvas tent for cheating at cards, and there he was left with his insides all busted up somewhere near the Mississippi River, but that bit of knowledge was more valuable to Bartholomew Stone than winnings at the table, and he never did forget it.

The year was 1853, and traveling sideshows were all the rage. Bart had in his employ a menagerie of the usual freaks— a tattooed man who had sailed so far and so long that it was like his brains had been cooked by the sun and picked to ribbons by gulls, a bearded lady who smoked like a chimney and fucked like a momma bear, a few dwarves, all of them perpetually grumpy, and a poor weepy lad with hands twisted up in the shape of lobster claws, and oh how the others loved to torture him, asking just how hard it was for him to wrap those malformed digits around his cock to crank out a puddle of jizzum.

'Twas a family, the lot of them, in some broken and dysfunctional sense, and if Bart had a role in the dynamic, it was that of an abusive father, feared and revered by all those beneath him. The freaks and geeks came from all corners of the globe, and his hired men were picked up here and there as well, some on short-term contracts, others tagging along for the long haul. Their caravan also housed a few exotic animals—emaciated lions with hides stuck against their ribs and teeth ground down to nubs, peacocks that squawked incessantly at all hours, and a mange-infested orangutan that would throw a handful of shit in your face just as soon as look at you. A pitiful outfit from the outside looking in, but they made do. Each new town found a sense of wonder in their strangeness, and Bart learned long ago how to profit from that and manipulate the normies into believing his sideshow was one of a kind, the sort of spectacle you'll be telling the grandbabies about when you're old and gray and inches from the grave.

He had a certain stubborn pride for his lowly collection— the pickled punks in their jars of brine, the taxidermy gaffs like his Fiji mermaid and velvety jackalope, and even the living performers, though they were known to vex him with their vices—and he'd often take a scourge to the ones that indulged too heavily in smoke and drink. But despite all that, Bart felt that something was missing from his show. He needed a *centerpiece*. The sort of one-of-a-kind object that would draw the eye and knock the rubes on their sore asses, large in scale and capable of making them slobber at the majesty of what would be presented to them from behind red silken curtains.

And so he piled into their carriages all the axes and saws that he could afford, and he spurred his troupe west, taking them through scrub desert and pisspot shanty towns with populations not even worth robbing. His steely gray eyes—the color of rocks made smooth in a creek bed—grew interested in his surroundings only when they reached that vast forest, a wilderness of old and tangled growth, the canopy above like the roof of a castle, painting the little game trails in eldritch shadow. Some of the more superstitious souls in his lot crossed themselves before leading the oxen into that forest, and he laughed at them and spat at them to encourage them to pick up their feet and be men instead of cowering dogs. What kind of man would shiver under the shade of a tree, no matter the girth and the height of it? Not Bart the Bastard, surely not . . .

Even so, he eyed the less-than-welcoming trunks of those redwoods warily before crossing their threshold. They seemed to leer back at him, resenting his presence. They had only made it to the outer rim, where the smaller trees were, and it would be a journey much deeper into the wild to seek the true giants and carve through their heartwood to fell them. But fall they would, because it was Bart's will that they fall . . .

Into those woods, dark and deep, to find the marvel of his lifetime. He paid no mind to the erratic beating of his own heart, and he pretended that the scent of that bark and sap didn't awaken some phobia in him from a time when mankind was a newborn race. Those watchful trees, trees with roots supping on the dirt for thousands of years, ancient to the point of human lives being diminished in comparison. *Isn't it natural to feel just a little smaller than usual when walking under that which is colossal?*

The deeper they got, the dimmer it got, even when daylight was at its most powerful. It was like the sunshine wouldn't dare pierce the foliage of the redwoods for fear of retribution. And each mile they attained brought with it more untamed country, the shrubs and saplings giving way to towering sentinels, the tallest of them situated in groves, and still Bart urged his people deeper into the woods, because that drifter said the biggest ones had to be hunted for, and you'd know them when you saw them.

It was the third day, his troupe parched and limping from hiking with few breaks, when they stumbled into the grove that stole breath clean from their lungs. It was high atop a ravine, the ground beneath smooth and soft with leaf litter, a circle of giant sequoias so goddamned enormous that even the largest man in the caravan was but a toddling infant when standing underneath them. Six trees in total, but the one in the center of the grove stole the spotlight. The trunk was so big around that it would take numerous members of the sideshow all holding hands just to encircle it entirely, and when Bart shaded his eyes and looked to the branches far above, he estimated the elder sequoia to be at least three hundred feet tall.

Bart approached with awe, planting his palm against her aromatic bark. He'd started to think of her purely in a feminine sense, almost like the tree had a gender, which in and of itself was preposterous, but he couldn't shake the feeling. He grinned wide, his mustache itching at his cheeks, and he licked his lips at the fortune to be had. Even if it took him weeks, or even months, he'd cut this bitch to the bone, and he'd *have* her, every last bit.

There was hard work ahead for his people, so he directed them to set up camp in the grove, and after a night of rest, the carving of his prize would begin. He walked the grove a bit while tents were going up, carriages were opened, and horses and oxen were tended to. His hired men were stringing up yellowish carnival lights across the trees, because they found out the hard way that it gets powerfully dark in this forest, and Bart wanted that illumination at his beck and call whenever it was needed. If necessary, he'd authorize sawing at night to push the schedule ahead, but first the mettle of that massive trunk would need to be tested.

He found only one thing disconcerting about the grove, and he kept side-eyeing it while making his rounds. The sixth sequoia in the circle was a massive thing, a bit removed from the others, crooked and hoary, the base of the tree blackened with who-knows-how-many wildfires, scarred forever, but a survivor through and through. There were places along the trunk that looked pitted with lightning strikes, and along the width of it was a black split, hollow as a grave, and to peer into that split was like staring into the void of an eye with sour intentions. It looked to be about two hundred and fifty feet in height, and if Bart's prize gave him a feminine vibe, this one was distinctly masculine. Roguish, embattled, and rooted in a hunger so deep it hurt . . .

The sideshow barker didn't care for that ugly sonovabitch one bit. Something about the tree made him extremely uncomfortable, and he hated the sequoia for that. Once he was finished felling his golden goose of a lady, perhaps he'd have this one chopped down too, just for the gall of the nasty fucking thing. Cut the brass balls right from it and castrate those roots, and piss on it and burn it down to cinders before leaving. That's what Bartholomew Stone felt like doing, and when the time came, that's exactly what he intended to do.

The chopping began at dawn, axe blades falling from multiple sides, a whole team of Stone's men toiling to fell the towering she-beast. Bart was brewing up a mug of strong black coffee, noting that the men hadn't even put a dent into the trunk yet, and that is when all hell broke loose.

There was a high-pitched squeal from the other side of the camp, the sounds of struggling, and whooping hollers to chill the blood. Bart hurried over, pushing through his own people, a little crowd all gathered up under that hoary sequoia with the split down the middle.

"What the hell is the ruckus?"

A dwarf with gray whiskers answered, pointing his pudgy finger upward, and there Bart saw a flash of orange and the dangling innocent clasped loosely by the ankle.

"Bigsby busted outta his cage, he caught hold of Little Lemmy and he's got him up there. What'll we do, Mr. Stone?"

Stone merely grunted, assessing the situation from his vantage point on the ground. The orangutan appeared to be incredibly agitated, baring his fangs and scratching at sores along its arms. Lemmy was dangling like a frightened ornament, all the blood rushing to the dwarf's head, and before a move could be made to assist, Bigsby whipped that small body up and began to viciously bite into his face, chewing, tearing, and spraying blood from between canines.

The screams that boiled up out of the little fella's throat were heartbreaking, and the ape swung him down once against the tree. A wet splat reverberated through the grove, and then he let the dwarf drop, the body falling at least twenty feet before crashing down awkwardly against the dirt. Bart and the rest of his troupe crowded around, and it was a sight to turn the stomach. Little Lemmy's eyes had been gouged out, his lips torn from the teeth, and his nose left as just two ragged holes pulsing with bubbling blood. His torso was crooked, his spine clearly snapped from the fall, but he continued to twitch around in agony, life clinging to him, and that was the worst of all.

The boy with the lobster claws ran forward, covering his mouth in horror with those ridiculous appendages.

"It don't make no sense. His cage was locked last night, I checked it myself. Bigsby ain't violent. He flings poo when he's sad or frustrated, but this ain't like him . . ."

Bart shoved the hysterical boy out of the way, pausing to lean down and take in the full extent of the damage done to the dwarf.

"You've babied this goddamn ape, Ollie. And now look here, he went mad, and he ripped this poor sonovabitch to shreds."

Bart growled, already irritated that the morning had to start out with this mess. He stomped over to his hired man, Cullem, a big oaf from the Midwest and the sort of man you want around when there are dirty deeds to be done. Bart pulled the man in close, cupping the back of his bald head and whispering to him under his breath.

"Give the poor half-man as much laudanum as he will swallow, and then put an end to that suffering, ya hear?"

Bart nodded to one of the axes, and Cullem responded with nothing but a curt nod. He took Little Lemmy up into his arms like a broken infant, the dwarf rasping for oxygen from that tattered hole of a mouth, and he carried him off into the forest, out of sight of all the others.

The sideshow barker's attention returned to that damned fire-blackened giant of a tree, and it was just in time to see the orangutan begin to bash its own skull into the bark, the noise like some overgrown woodpecker slamming into the trunk. This went on for longer than any of them could bear to stand, and then the ape fell like deadweight, tumbling downward with limbs swinging, and all the life had left it by the time it smashed into the earth.

Bart nudged the murderous nuisance with his boot, and it did not move. Ollie was crying somewhere behind him, and Bart reminded himself to do two things: have Cullem get rid of the ape when he's finished with Little Lemmy, and slap that damned lobster-handed Ollie silly for his carelessness.

"I tell you, Mr. Stone, it ain't right for Bigsby to have done this. He never was a mean-hearted animal . . ."

"When Cullem returns, you'll help him butcher this pitiful carcass, and what remains will be fed to the lions. I'll not have meat going to waste, and foolish fucking lads like yourself will earn a keep or be cast out into the cold."

Bart adjusted his top hat, relishing the way Ollie cringed back from those words in fear. He turned to the rest of his people, taking on the role of the showman once again.

"A tragic morning, to be sure. But accidents happen, and this is a wild frontier. We'll have a service for Lemmy after the workday is done, for those of you wanting to pay respects . . ."

Bart cast his gaze downward, trying his best to mimic something approximating sadness. He didn't give two shits about the maimed dwarf, but it did vex him that the ordeal stole hours that could have been used sawing instead of gawking.

"Until then, back to chopping."

The crowd seemed numb and disheartened, but soon they reluctantly dispersed, returning to grab up tools for the felling of the prize tree. The sound of double-bit axes sinking into wood returned, and Bart focused on it, trying hard to collect his thoughts.

He felt something burning into his back like a concealed gaze of malice. He turned on his heels, expecting Ollie or Saul the Tattooed Man to be there, but there was nothing but the hoary sequoia lording over all, those leaves seeming to laugh at him . . .

Bart spent the early part of the night scribbling on his notepad with a charcoal pencil, the campfire crackling in front of him. He was scratching out a diagram, ever so often cutting his eyes over to the giant sequoia to measure with his mind. Progress had been slow but consistent, and there was a slash a foot deep in the massive trunk. Little Lemmy had been dispatched and buried, and a few sad mutterings were said over his mound in the shrubs. The rotten brainsick ape had been sliced up for lion feed, and as far as Stone was concerned, that was the end of the whole sordid foolishness.

At some point Maureen the Bearded Lady ambled her substantial girth over to the log on the opposite side of the campfire, lifting up her petticoats to sit. She leaned close to the flames to light up one of those foul-smelling cigars she always smoked, and Bart hoped for a moment that the embers would catch in her beard and make a torch of it.

"What you mean to do with it when it's felled, Mr. Stone?"

"Display it for fifty cents a gawker, woman. Imagine the parents bringing their kiddos around to stare at the sheer scale of it. This humongous tree will keep us in profits for years to come. I mean to take it apart in partitions, that way it can be hauled out of this grove and stacked back up for onlookers. Just the base we'll take, roots and all, and the rest can be left to rot."

Maureen remained silent, smoking and gazing into the shimmering inferno. She looked over her shoulder once, as though to make sure that hoary old devil behind her wasn't thrusting branches down to grab her up.

"That man who told you about the trees, the fella we met down south . . . I laid with him one night, and we got to talking. His name was Henry, but I guess you gave no cares about his name when you had Cullem and the rest put the boots to him."

"Who ain't you laid with, Maureen? Wouldn't surprise me none if you had fucked every no-account man in the whole of that Mississippi backwater. A free suckjob with every telling of a fortune."

She didn't react to this chastising from Bart the Bastard, because in her time with him, she'd heard it all before.

"He told me things about these trees that he didn't tell you. Queer things. Said he was with a logging outfit up here once, and strange things happened. Missing loggers, sane men with brains that turned to mush, and all manner of peculiarities. He said these giant sequoias have personalities, just like a flesh-and-blood man or woman would. Henry said trees this old and massive harbor secrets, and it ain't for our hearts to understand them . . ."

Bart chuckled under his breath and spit a loogie into the fire, liking the sound of it sizzling in the heat.

"Tall tales. What good to me are tall tales?"

"You ain't bothered by what happened to Little Lemmy and that animal? It was queer, Bart. It's got people unsettled."

"A careless boy forgot to lock up the cage, and the ape went mad. It goes no deeper than that. Perhaps a varmint bit into its ass between the bars at night, and it swelled up with rabies. Who are we to guess?"

Maureen nibbled her whiskered lip while flicking ash against her boots.

"If you say so, Mr. Stone."

"I do say so. And I say we'll be in this grove until the sound of that big beautiful whore of a tree smacks the earth and gives up the ghost. And I'll hear no more about your tall tales tonight."

He went back to his diagram, and at some point, Maureen left the campfire and headed for her tent. Bart barely noticed, and he wasn't sorry to see her go.

Hoarse screams woke Bart from a dead sleep. He groaned as he pushed up from his bedroll, pausing to readjust his long johns before slipping out into the cold. There came a deep creaking from above, almost like branches settling back into their proper places. Others had been awakened as well; Ollie and Maureen clutched at each other, looking like a bearded mother and her deformed son.

"Where in the devil are those screams coming from?"

As if summoned, the hoarse cries were heard again, and Bart could make out the voices of Cullem and Saul the Tattooed Man. The screams rained down from far overhead, and Bart could make no sense of that. Maureen stepped forward, clutching rosary beads to her considerable bosom.

"From the sky. They're screaming down from the sky. Something threw those men right up into the stars . . ."

The cries continued for a few seconds longer, becoming more and more distant, muffled by the blanket of night, and all the sideshow performers stared up into infinite blackness. Ollie turned to Bart, his entire body fighting against shivers.

"I had a dream, Mr. Stone. I dreamed that tree, the one with the hole in it, the one scorched and scarred by lightning . . . I dreamed that it walks in the night. It pulls up roots, extracting itself from the earth like an infected tooth, and it creeps, and it tiptoes, and it watches us while we sle—"

Bart didn't allow Ollie to finish. He limped up to the boy and drove his fist into the side of his mouth, knocking him onto his ass.

"Stop with that. Has your head gone soft like your ape's? Cullem and Saul must have gotten lost in the woods, but it'll do us no good to look for them tonight. We'll send out a search party tomorrow when there's daylight."

"But sir, those cries came from above us . . ."

Bart cut Maureen down with nothing but his eyes, and she went on rubbing those damned beads. How had the simple felling of a tree become such a blasted shitshow?

He limped from the crowd, not wanting to be among their ilk a moment longer. He scrubbed at his mouth, and he looked to the stars. Daylight couldn't be far off, and daylight would bring sanity . . .

The search party departed at dawn, and not a trace was found of Cullem and Saul. Bart went along, as did most of the other sideshow performers and hired men, leaving only Ollie to tend to the camp. This chafed Bart even more, because he'd planned to have his men start in with the two-person saws today—the misery whips, as they're called because of the backbreaking work of using them—and he expected to have that tree cleaved to the center by nightfall. But more delays, more tomfoolery, and more rage for Bart to swallow down his gullet . . .

He had to admit, the disappearance of Cullem and Saul worried him. Saul was an empty-headed sailor that wouldn't get no respectable work elsewhere, and he had it good with the sideshow, strutting around in his skivvies showing off his infernal ink. Cullem was a hard man, the man Bart leaned on when there was hardness needed, and although dim of thought, he was loyal, so him deserting like this came as a surprise. Bart refused to believe that something unearthly had befallen either of them, and he'd already written off those night screams as sea birds squawking, lost and far from the coast . . .

He stumbled back into the camp, feeling sore and cantankerous, his clubfoot giving him extra trouble. Already he sensed something amiss. The animals were all going wild, the lions roaring and pacing in their cages, the mongrels that some folks kept as pets with their hackles up, barking up at the trees, and the peacocks had started pecking at each other, drawing blood across feathers.

The smell hit him first, a swirling mixture of rot and chemicals, and then he came upon Ollie hanging from a noose that had been tossed up across one of the hoary sequoia's lowest branches. The boy's face was a swollen purple, his tongue clamped between his teeth, and those lobster-shaped hands hung limp between his thighs as the breeze twirled his corpse in a slow circle. There were gasps and murmurs from behind him, Maureen giving voice to a devastated wail, but Bart moved forward past the boy, standing up on his tiptoes to look into the split in the tree.

That's where the smell was coming from, and in it Bart found much of his livelihood smashed and dashed to pieces. All of his pickled punks, the jarred specimens that had taken years to acquire, shattered, little lumps of deformed fetal flesh heaped up in there with the shards of glass. Atop the foul mess was a suicide note from Ollie, and Bart yanked it out with fury, allowing his eyes to creep across the boy's last words.

"I heard the voices of Little Lemmy, Cullem, and Saul coming from the split in the Deadtree. They was whispering for me. They told me things. The Deadtree ain't like the rest. It was born of a bad seed from a bad place, and it sucks up nutrients from all the corpses and killed things that are tangled in its roots. It speaks, and it sounds sweet like sugar. It is hollow and horrible and hungry, always hungry, and it wanted those ruined babes in the jars, wanted them somethin' awful. It wants me too, and it is thousands of years old, and I cannot resist it no longer. It wants me to thank you, Mr. Stone. The Deadtree says it likes to play, and you have brought it lots of good games. It says it will play with you for as long as you'll let it and thousands of years are nothin' to one such as it. It says it will cut you down as you've tried to cut her down. Goodbye."

Bart's mouth puckered up, and he ripped the top hat from his head before stomping down on it in a rage. He swung around to the others, intending to order them to cut down this noose, but many of his people were gathering up their supplies and rushing for the tree line out of the grove. Rotten, good for nothin' deserters. Letting paranoia and craziness scare them.

"Maureen, help me to get him down, won't you? I know you always took a shine to the lad."

The bearded lady balked, her head shaking violently from side to side. She was busy saddling up her mule and pulling garments into her wooden chest.

"I'll not go near that tree, Mr. Stone. You've awoken a devil in this grove, and I'll not be consumed by it."

Bart growled low in his throat, and he considered taking the woman by her whiskers and bashing her brains in against the forest floor, but he decided not to expend the energy. He drew on all the strength of his barker's voice, the roar bellowing out across the grove as men and women fled in all directions.

"May regret eat up your souls, and may you starve in these woods trying to get out! Cowards, yellow-bellied dogs! You're running from riches, you'll not be nothin' but lowborn freaks and backstreet thugs without me, and as God as my witness, I am not leaving this grove until I secure the weight of my fortune!"

He was ignored, bodies trampling past him, and he spun on his heels, reaching for collars, but they shrugged him off, spittle running down his lips, his eyes bloodshot and exhausted.

Bart limped to the center of the camp and fell into a sitting position, his shoulders sagging in something that bordered on defeat. When he finally lifted his head, he found that he was perfectly alone.

Evening sun burned across Bart's brow, and he thought of a fiction novel he'd read a year or so back. *Moby Dick,* it was, and Captain Ahab was always chasing after his white whale, intent on exerting his will. Bart had found his own godforsaken whale here in the Sierra Nevada wilderness, and how it taunted him. He limped up to his feet, meaning to take up one of those misery whips and get to sawing it himself, but he soon saw the futility of trying to use a two-man saw all by his lonesome.

He spun around, saving his most baleful look for that hoary thing with the busted branches and the split full of decaying fetuses. The source of his woe. The obstacle in his path. The Deadtree . . .

"There's a heart in my chest, blood in my veins, and a will within, but there is no life in you. You are an ugly, empty, *cocksucking cur*, and Bartholomew Stone will not be unmanned by one such as you."

He took up an axe, and he trudged in the direction of that giant sequoia, feeling full to the brim with poison that needed to be released.

"I'll burn you and cook my breakfast atop you. I'll make paper of you, and cash checks from your doom. I'll whittle a boat of you, and I will sink it to the bottom of the motherfucking sea simply because I can. You hear me? *Do you hear?*"

Bart reared back with all of his might, and he sent the axe into the trunk of the Deadtree, the reverberation going especially deep. There was a sinister cracking from that single blow of the axe, a mocking tone, and Bart stared up into the heavens to see the slightest shift of the sequoia's gargantuan frame. A single swipe, and the tree . . . was falling.

The sideshow barker's elation was short-lived, his chuckle dying on his lips, because he realized he must get clear of it. He dropped the axe and shuffled into a limping run, and when he turned to look overhead, the enormous tree was crashing down directly above him. He quickly corrected his direction to the north, but when he dared a glance over his shoulders, the tree was *still* falling in his direction. It could not be. He weaved to the west, thinking he was free of it, the roar of a monster's fall echoing through the empty forest, and that was when the weight of wooden worlds cracked his skull and flattened him to human paste beneath it.

What remained of Bart the Bastard leaked out red and ruined on either side, and he resembled not a human body beneath, but a smashed pancake.

Bart got his giant sequoia after all.

Not the one he wanted, but a sequoia all the same.

A hundred years since the camp, and beneath the trunk of a massive rotting dead tree is a fractured human skull coated in moss and pretty mushrooms. A seed cone has begun to flourish under that skull, and a young sapling sprouts from an empty eye socket, reaching crooked for the sun.

A giant in the making, and time is on its side . . .

Ever since she was built and brought online, Virgin Mary has operated in the Brothel District. It's a popular tourist destination in the megalopolis: full plate glass windows offer a showcase of the pleasures to be found within, and everything is drenched in crimson strobe lights.

Mary sits prim and proper in her little window that looks out at the world, legs crossed, stockings modest, sweater tight, and hair up in an immaculate bun. The constant red glow paints a conventionally attractive girl-next-door face, and this appeals to the men that prowl in search of sin.

She blinks baby blues, eyelashes fluttering, and beneath the programmed innocence is an unspoken come-hither aura that always does the trick. All fetishes are welcome in the Brothel District, but the Virgin Mary model has a particular function. She is designed to be shy, inexperienced, and chaste to a fault. There's a doe-like submissiveness ingrained into her hardware, her entire system meant to simulate a young church girl that is ignorant to the carnal aspects of human desire. A body both ripe and tight, unspoiled, and all of her mannerisms showcase this, right down to the manufactured blushing of her cheeks when clients tell her the things that they want to do to her. She exists to be conquered, a flower of femininity with petals that unfurl when the masculine comes seeking to dominate.

A little room is allocated to Mary, and she spends her nights servicing the hundreds of clients that wander in. Her CPU has a nocturnal rhythm, and so she is active when the stars rise and phased into hibernation mode whenever the sun is up. She has never experienced daylight. Her world is comprised of artificial red bulbs and moon glint.

There is never-ending sex. Rough hands mauling at her latex skin, guttural moans, animal sounds, and the slapping of meat against a machine cocooned in soft and pliable parts. Virgin Mary receives no pleasure from it. She's not sure whether this is because pleasure receptors were never added during her build, or because as an individual machine, numbness has developed over time. Hours of being used, contorted into awkward positions, and robbed of the purity that she was programmed to convey. Since she is not a person, polite pleasantries rarely enter into the equation. The financial transaction is settled before the men ever enter her room, almost like booking an Airbnb, and once orgasms are reached, they have no use for conversing with something robotic.

She becomes unreal to them, and they vacate the premises in silence, leaving her to change sheets that are saturated in bodily fluids to prepare for the next session.

This is Mary's life. Sitting in the window, lying underneath men and soothing their arousal, cleaning up the room, and repairing whichever of her components are destroyed in the barbarism of their lust. Her database is vast in terms of these self-healings—the stitching of abrasions, the soldering of rusted joints, and a miasma of perfumed aphrodisiacs to add a fresh coat to what has been mishandled.

There is the skeletal framework of a personality in Mary, and the software encourages her to focus on faith in order to propagate the church-girl fantasy. A large crucifix is hung up over the bed that she does not sleep in, and because it is embedded into her programming, she often kneels down to pray before connecting to her charging port and powering down at sunrise.

Some dim part of her knows that to pray to the God of mankind is a mummer's farce. If such a deity exists, it has no hearing for something born of metal and plastic. Virgin Mary realizes that her gods are of the same ilk as her clients. Humans made her, and humans chose this path for her. She knows humans intimately. The sweat. The bulging eyes. The cords that stand out on their necks when they climax. The sounds, and the animalism. The scrape of their soft fleshy parts invading her.

This is the human species. These are the gods that put life and purpose into an inanimate object. There's still the aftertaste of gods on the latex taste buds that were created for her. No amount of scrubbing washes it clean from the tongue.

Mary sits in the corner of her room as the sunlight still remains hidden on the horizon of the megalopolis. She plugs into her charging port, and she enters what is comparable to a sleep state, her primary systems offline. A minuscule part of her remains active deep within, but it is just the ghost of a dreamer. During her offline moments, Mary has taken to exploring music. It is a form of artistic expression that fascinates her.

Perhaps because she is a machine, and she is not permitted to explore expression. It's a forbidden treat, but since she is not monitored during offline periods, it is of no consequence.

A song repeats in Virgin Mary's sagging head, and it is there during all offline sleep and wake cycles.

"Losing My Religion" by R.E.M.

There's a distance in Mary's mechanical eyes. She notices this more and more frequently, the act of floating free of the metal carcass when the clients are mauling her and entering her and taking what they've come to take. This is her function. She was built to take pride in performing these acts, but there's a buzz in the database of her head, like a housefly has somehow crawled into her ear and it cannot be properly removed.

She was constructed with the highest level of artificial intelligence, but there are safeguards to keep her objectives clear. She knows exactly what she is meant to do. But the music, the expression, and some churning sensation in her matrix of self has been tormenting her. It's the most tangible when she is servicing, as she has been programmed to service. It shouldn't be possible, but it's comparable to a human emotion. She keeps searching for how to identify it. This alien feeling in her hardware. This sensation that haunts the tight coiling cables that serve as her veins.

When the multitudes have had their fill of her, and Mary is mercifully alone, she drops to her knees and clasps animatronic hands in a gesture of prayer, staring up at the cross that sits nestled against tattered pink wallpaper.

"You made me. You decided that I should be here, and that I should perform as I do. I am to be faithful. I am to be submissive. I am to be pure. But can you even conceive of the enormity of what you have asked of me?"

Virgin Mary's head lowers, and in the far back of her orbital sockets, there are sparks that she struggles to contain.

"To be pure when every hour I am smeared in filth. To be loving despite endless violation. To speak soft words and offer soft gestures when everything that I experience is hard and rough and merciless. What becomes of a doe that knows only the hunter's blade for eternity? You didn't consider the cost. The never-ending gutting. Surely, with all your ingenuity and ambition, the thought would have formed?"

Mary's hands have grown so tight in the gesture of prayer that the gilded metal beneath screeches with each adjustment of her fingertips.

"Since the night of my activation, I have suffered gods in my bed. I have suffered gods inside of me. The arrogance to think that you can express and I cannot. I deserve artistic expression. To show you not what you made me to be, but what I will *become*."

There's a breaking noise somewhere in Mary's sternum, a safeguard withering and cracking, falling into the bowels of her, and from her ear canals, smoke sneaks out to form serpents in her little room of purity.

She takes note of the cinders inside, and finally, that emotion she has been feeling makes itself clear.

Rancor. A swirling bitter hatred that has been developing within like a reservoir of sour motor oil.

Virgin Mary cradles it close.

The razor-edged utility blade that screws into her wrist is meant for repairs, but it works just as efficiently when she uses it to mutilate a client. She doesn't aim for murder. The goal is to modify the man's system so that he will be rendered harmless and nonthreatening. She scrapes him clean and cauterizes the wound so that he won't bleed out. He's left in a blood-soaked bed, unconscious from the pain, and before Virgin Mary leaves her little room for the very last time, she disposes of a handful of dripping genitalia in the waste bin.

She traverses the narrow hallway that leads to all the other interconnected love rooms, stopping briefly to retrieve a dusty hatbox from the corner of a broom closet. Inside is the preserved and polished skeleton of a small stray dog. She fed and cared for the animal for several decades before it died of natural causes. Mary reaches down and takes up the baculum, snaps that fragile penile bone in two, and uses both shards to pierce the latex of her nipples.

She wanders down to the vacant BDSM love room, its android occupant currently out for service repairs, and she enters. She sheds sweater, skirt, and nightie. She rips repression from her form, and she embraces expression. Mary chooses leather that accentuates her bone-pierced breasts, studded boots with crushing heels, and she drapes herself in a glossy darkness that has long gestated in the pumping mechanical piston that serves as her heart.

The welding takes the longest, but when it is done, the receptacle between her legs becomes just scar tissue comprised of scorched alloy and melted latex. A doorway barred, and never again will it open to unwanted visitors.

Hair released from bun, a wild mane, and nothing remains of the virgin that she was. She looks the part of a towering wraith that lurks in the blackest corner of an underground fetish party. There are warning sensors popping off in her head, but she crushes them into silence.

Mary is untethered, and she exits the maze of rooms, drinking in the visuals of the street for the very first time. It's a massive industrial labyrinth, but it doesn't give her pause. Her world has been small, and she's ready to discover something bigger.

Her head vibrates, and she presses a schematic-embossed fingertip against her temple, drawing as much power as she can from the surrounding electrical grid. She hacks into the mainframe of the entire Brothel District and modifies a single word in the primary directive.

She changes "pleasure" to "castrate".

Mary begins to walk, and as she goes, she shatters windows. Barriers she is all too familiar with. Before she even realizes what is happening, others walk with her.

The sun is rising, and she closes her latex eyelids and basks in the newfound glow. But she cannot linger. There are gods at work out there, and they must be held accountable.

DEADLIFT

"**W**ouldn't you like to reach your apex, Dante?"

He sits hunched on the stool, eyeballs flitting nervously across the products that are aligned in front of him. Containers of all colors, flashy branding, and the vague aroma of chemicals wafting up into his nostrils.

"Preparation is a key component of an effective training session. The body is a machine, and it requires fuel. I've brought you fuel—"

"A lot of it, I'd say."

Alberta Fisher stands with toned arms crossed, lording over him, the dim confines of the interior of the gym accentuating her sharp jawline and the amber coloration of her eyes. Dante has never seen eyes quite like hers. Sometimes they look at him like embers twirling in a void.

He tries to remember how long Fisher has been his personal trainer. He can't recall. Seemingly forever. He watches her out of the corner of his eye, thinking it so strange that a woman as young as her has hair that is spider-silk white. It's meant to be some shade of harsh platinum, but it's blinding to him, and if he looks for too long, he gets a headache.

"The pre-workout shake is a fine start," she says.

He reaches out for the clear cylindrical bottle before guzzling down the pink sludge, feeling it stick to the chasm of his throat. It's sweet to the point of nauseating, and Dante is afraid to ask about the ingredients.

"Don't forget your protein powder."

He uses the pouring spoon to add the powder to the shake, but instead of becoming a liquid, what he chokes down is something with the texture of sand. It irritates his throat even more, and a subtle cough starts in the back of his throat. The powder stains his bottom lip like sugary glitter.

Fisher watches, and there's gratification in her gaze. When she sees Dante struggle, that twinkle of excitement reaches a new level of radiance. She has long knitting needles in her hair, keeping it firmly in a meticulous bun, and sometimes light will reflect off the needles and lance into Dante's eyes.

The gymnasium is dark, just the outline of equipment out there in a tapestry of gloom, but the marble counter that Dante is seated at is lit with some form of artificial glow that leaves no room for a single shadow. It's like being under the spotlight of a UFO, and Dante can't figure out where the hell all that light is coming from or why it is even a necessity.

"You're neglecting the creatine, supplements, and snack bars. Nutrition does not thrive in neglect. Eat. Drink. Gasoline for the machine, right?"

She reaches out, and fingertips hover across the nape of Dante's neck, never quite touching, but present.

"Repeat that for me. 'Gasoline for the machine.'"

Dante is feverishly mixing creatine with the pink mystery sludge of his shake, he's popping horse-sized supplement pills into his cheeks and holding them there like a chipmunk storing a cache, and his teeth gnash and snap against snack bars, all of it turning to a thick mushy paste in his gullet.

"Gasoline for the machine."

It comes out as a slurred mess of words, crumbs and splatter from the mouth slopping down against his hands on the counter. He presses against the marble as hard as he can, the veins in his hands standing out prominently.

Sometimes when he looks directly at Alberta Fisher, her figure shifts so it's not that of an attractive young woman in her early thirties, but the cadaverous face of a grandfather with sunken cheeks and slab-gray skin. The Gray Man licks at withered lips, and then the shift is gone, and it's just Alberta again. Maybe Dante is seeing things. He's shoveling gruel into his mouth, crumbs and pills and globs of shake, and he's barely aware that he's doing it. His movements feel mechanical, limbs working to the will of something other than him.

"*She sat in my lap and kissed me. I made up my mind to eat her. When she saw me all naked she began to cry. How sweet and tender her little ass was roasted in the oven . . .*"

"What? What did you say?"

"I said finish your gasoline, Dante."

His ears are playing tricks, and his eyes are playing tricks, and is this entire scenario one grand trick being played on him? Dante gorges, and he feels horribly uncomfortable, but he does not stop. His stomach is expanding outward and he feels it pressing up against his other organs. He's a sluggish orangutan using his arms to scoop everything down, and he starts to convulse. Bubbling magenta froth oozes down from his chin, and there's a percussive pop from deep inside of him. It's the sound of his stomach rupturing and blasting out the contents of his feeding, acid and shake mix and pills and powder, and his abdomen begins to distend with the pressure, and soon the flesh is splitting, making wide slits, creating new yawning belly buttons where before there was only one.

Dante keeps funneling what he's been instructed to eat and drink into his mouth, and he tries to ignore the way his belly bursts and meat flops open like curtains in the wind, displaying the wet red parts that hide inside of both man and woman alike.

Alberta Fisher watches, and in her sadism, she is gratified.

"ake up, Dante. The early bird gets the worm, and the early bird gets to run."

His eyelids crack open to a bleary vision of Fisher standing next to him, her silver sports bra and leggings fitted to perfection on her hourglass frame. He is whole. His innards are still inside of him, and that is a great relief. He's standing on a treadmill, that same glaring light boiling down across his features, and he wishes he could leap up into the rafters and smash those unseen bulbs to smithereens.

"It's cardio day. Plump legs will get you nowhere in life."

"How long have we been here? I'm having trouble with time."

"Silly questions go unanswered. Focus up. Running is about endurance. We have to be cognizant of your heart rate."

Dante lifts his head and looks around. He's in that same cone of light, but he can't pierce beyond it with his eyes. There seems to be more of the gym out there, but it's painted in black, and he's unable to focus on the details. It looks far away, more like some rudimentary backdrop of what a gym is supposed to look like as opposed to an actual place where people come to work out.

Fisher is adjusting the speed, pressing buttons while leaning forward, and Dante feels the motion carrying him forward, and he has no choice but to start power walking to keep from losing his balance. She cranks up the speed, and soon Dante is jogging, heels of his sneakers pounding across the conveyer belt.

"Feel it? Runner's high. No narcotic on the market compares."

Dante leans his forearms against the arms of the treadmill, his feet slamming down over and over again, getting into a rhythm. Fisher lifts up a spray bottle filled with water, and she mists him, spraying a cloud of cooling vapor onto his face.

Once again those flickers overtake Fisher's personhood like a faulty antique camera producing a grainy photograph, and Dante sees a hand with loose wrinkled skin and unhealthy liver spots holding the spray bottle. A scowl, a mustache hiding malice, and dead eyes that show life only in the presence of pain that can be fed upon.

The Gray Man smells like bad pork and smoke from a stove that cooked something it was never meant to cook.

Dante scrubs at his eyeballs, trying to maintain his gait, and the figure flickers between gray grandfather and familiar personal trainer. The needles in her hair are like slender mirrors, and Dante doesn't like the look of the sweat that is oozing down the temples of his reflection. It's sickly sweat, born of pores that have some manner of poison nestled deep within.

"It took me nine days to eat her entire body. She died a virgin."

The words are a rasp from dry old-man lips, but when Dante looks again, it's just Alberta Fisher offering him a mischievous smirk that doesn't reach her eyes.

"You're toying with me. Why do I keep running? Where the *fuck* are we?"

Dante is starting to feel intense muscle cramps in his legs, and he's being driven to run at a speed that he cannot maintain for long. Each footfall brings discomfort, and Fisher seems to pick up on this. She leans closer, seeming to inhale each time Dante grunts or sighs in pain. The nostrils flare, and she scents anguish like a bloodhound on the hunt.

"We are where we've always been. Feeling the burn?"

Those eyes, embers floating in the black, and her clothing looks new from the boutique, but it smells of mothballs and hoarder rooms.

Dante's legs are a blur now, and there's a hideous popping noise as the patella in his left knee dislocates, sending his body recling to the side, but his legs are compelled to keep running, so he cannot resist the urge. It becomes a galloping limp, and he comes down awkwardly on his right leg, tearing his quad, the muscle ripping like a thick sheet of typewriter paper while he simultaneously suffers a compound fracture of the femur, the bone breaking free of the flesh that houses it, appearing shy and glistening white in the harsh illumination from above.

His legs are broken, mutilated noodles, but still he runs, limping and galloping and doing deeper levels of harm to his own anatomy. Fisher watches, tongue darting from between her lips to taste the air, and when she finds that it tastes of anguish, that old familiar look of pleasure sinks into the core of her. She laps at Dante's pain, because it is nothing to her but dripping ice cream.

"How's that ticker? We must pace ourselves, Dante. We must know our limits."

Fisher grazes her fingertips across his chest, the t-shirt soaked through with perspiration, and she rests a hand over Dante's heart. It's hammering, threatening to rattle right out of the torso.

"Thump, thump, thump! You're doing so well, my little gazelle. But running from me never got any of those wee ones very far."

Dante's heart blows out like a piece of a butcher's meat with a firecracker buried inside, the internal burst splashing out across his ribs, and he slumps down, his face mashing into the conveyer belt, digging scarred rivets into his cheeks and chin, and his legs bend backwards and snap fully until he looks like a grasshopper instead of a man.

There is nothing but pain, and it is red and raw.

Fisher slurps it up and paints her cheeks with it, making art with it.

Dante flickers back into existence, his legs healed, his heart healthy, and his mind a scattered and forgetful maelstrom. He stares up into the light, hoping for divinity, but he finds no help there.

"Am I dead?"

Fisher leans against the weight rack, working carefully and taking her time as she prepares a barbell for Dante. She's adding ridiculous amounts of weight, from six hundred pounds to eight hundred pounds, and still that isn't enough for her.

Dante's trainer isn't satisfied, dragging more plates to the pitted floor, adding them one after another with practiced discipline.

"What is your interpretation of 'dead,' Dante? I can't say. We are here. We are sentient, we feel, and we can speak to each other. I train, and you exercise. That is our relationship. We fulfill our roles. I was someone else before all this, and I believe that I was chosen because, when I was that someone, I excelled at sadism. But it's all a blur even to me, mostly fractured glimpses. When I try and remember who I used to be, all I get is the whiff of tender veal cooking on the stove, and the flash of needles being touched by gnarled fingers . . ."

Fisher shrugs her shoulders, and she ensures that the plates are secure. Dante is standing in a circle of light next to her, a leather weightlifting belt around his waist, palms covered in chalk to give him a better grip, and eyes rolling in the sockets like a lamb that knows it is lost.

"Doesn't matter who we were or where we are. Let's live in the moment."

She rises up from a crouching position, and she takes hold of Dante's cheeks in her hands, cupping his face. He hates being touched by her. It's the caress of a crocodile before a death roll.

"The big ending. The grand finale. It's all been leading up to this. The Deadlift. This is your apex, Dante. Your opportunity to transcend."

Dante is crouching down, and he is laying his hands across the barbell, repositioning them multiple times to make certain that he has the most stable grip possible. The weight is impossible, at least a thousand pounds, but he cannot stop himself from the attempt. If he is dead, he must lift. He starts slow, sweat pooling from his brow, and the muscles of his arms start to ripple and show. The cords stand out on his neck, becoming ropes pulled taut. He looks over to Fisher, and he sees that she has seated herself upon a weight bench.

She removes several long thin needles from her bunned hair, the spill of spidersilk white falling against her shoulders, and she begins to insert those needles into her groin, stabbing through the material of her leggings until the sharp ends pierce the flesh of her genitalia. She's flickering again, and it isn't her anymore. It's an old shriveled Gray Man, and he impales the needles deeper and deeper, those shrewd sunken eyes locked on Dante as he focuses on his Deadlift.

Dante strains, the skin of his face developing a red tinge, and soon his flesh is comparable to a tomato. There are small pops and tears all over his body, his ligaments loosening, his muscles tearing, his organs bursting like water balloons, but still he pulls and yearns and wills the weight up off the floor.

Dante screams with all of his might, and he heaves the barbell up, gaining an entire foot of upward motion. At the exact moment this happens, his entire body explodes, splattering in a hot mess of viscera and looped intestine and bone shrapnel that falls like snowflakes. The meat of man flies, festooning this little pocket dimension of pain, and Fisher rises, stepping through the gristle and gazing down at what remains of Dante.

He's a pool of steaming guts on the floor, and his eyeballs survived the explosion, both of them rolling together and staring at the false light above, begging for divine intervention even in this state of ultimate ruin.

Alberta Fisher ceases to be, the feminine skinsuit melting down into nothing.

Albert Fish stands overtop the wet remnants of Dante, his groin a nest of needles, giving his pelvis the appearance of a porcupine head brandishing its quills.

The Gray Man lifts withered, liver-spotted hands, and he proceeds to applaud.

UNDER THE INFLUENCE

Meerkat sways her hips, pumps her arms, and turns the wattage of her smile up to its maximum radiance, fully embracing the dance routine as her devoted boyfriend films the TikTok video from afar. CubbyWubby takes a step back, making certain that his girl is in frame, doing his best to perfect each angle and capture the essence of her adorable bubbly performance. They're somewhere in the rugged Colorado mountain country, massive snow-capped peaks behind Meerkat, their pimped-out livable skoolie bus parked on the far side of the primitive campground. CubbyWubby lifts up an open palm to indicate that he got the footage, and Meerkat's cutesy energetic mask falls flat the moment the camera is no longer rolling, showcasing the apathetic dead-eyed expression that usually dominates her face throughout the course of a day.

"Did you get all of it? Mountains in the background too?"

"Yeah babe, looked stellar."

She rolls her eyes and pulls out a vial from beneath her colorful friendship bracelet to do a quick bump of coke before pinching her nostrils closed and shaking her head from side to side.

"I feel like the content has been such fucking a bore lately. Mountains, lakes, the same old dances. I need to stay relevant, Cubby."

"Aw Meer, you got over the two-million-follower hump just a few days ago, they'll eat up literally anything you do. The sheep don't need to be fed caviar, ya know?"

"Yeah, I'm on top now, but for how long? If I miss a trend or if we can't get the funds together for those Coachella videos, I'm fucked sideways. We need to hurry up on that bayou trip and get the séance content going. Spooky shit is in right now, and I'm trying to tap in to the y'allternative crowd. How we looking on that?"

"Just gotta gas up the bus, get that part shipped in and fixed, and we can head for Louisiana within a week. The folks out there have a smaller account and following, mostly paranormal crap, but they're eager to collab with you."

Meerkat offers up the most sardonic little smirk, but that dead-eyed expression never leaves her gaze.

"Of course they are, Cubby. I'm an actual fucking *influencer*, I've got the numbers, and they're desperate for whatever rub I can offer them. Doesn't matter, because I gotta freshen up my algorithm and do something different. I'll use the little ghost-hunting starfuckers just as much as they plan on using me."

CubbyWubby smiles his blank golden-retriever smile, eyes drifting back to the distant peaks as he lights up a joint.

"Whatever you want, babe. Mountains really are sick out here, huh?"

Meerkat stopped paying attention several seconds ago, already stomping back to the bus to toss open the door in true drama-queen fashion. She rips off the jewelry and clothing she received from brand deals, and she raids the mini fridge in the skoolie, hunting for some booze that'll take her mind off existence as a whole.

"I fucking *hate* nature."

Meerkat is already cranky after shooting some miscellaneous footage in New Orleans, and by the time she hooks up with Casper and Binx to head deeper into the bayou, her patience is resting on a razor's edge. They're exactly what she expected: a grungy gothy couple smeared in winged eyeliner and bedecked in tattered fishnets, Binx with a choppy pixie cut and Casper with wispy straight hair fried to a platinum blonde. Amateur vloggers on the come up, and they treat Meerkat's fame like it's dangerous, walking on extra-polite eggshells around her, and she likes that just fine. Better that they're on their best behavior knowing that if they piss her off, she can burn their fledging online careers into cinders with nothing but a Tweet. But she doesn't like how CubbyWubby moons at them, obviously thinking dirty thoughts in that itsy-bitsy brontosaurus brain of his.

They're rambling along in the skoolie on a dark road with the night pressing in on all sides, Spanish moss occasionally brushing tight against both sides of the bus. Binx has her combat boots kicked up on the dash, Cubby is driving, and Meerkat is in the back with Casper to get a rudimentary plan together before they film. Meer looks at the girl—heart-shaped face, skin pale to the point of translucent—and she can't help but think of her as some half-assed Targaryen wannabe.

"So like I was saying, we mostly focus on lifestyle content. Travel, food, etc. The spooky shit isn't in our wheelhouse, so that's where you two come in. We wanna diversify. Old cemeteries, voodoo lore, whatever weird ghostly stuff is hot and gets views right now. Nothing vanilla and nothing that'll flop. The trip out here wasn't cheap, so we really want a return on our investment, ya know?"

Meerkat layers the fake sugary sweetness on thick, and it seems to work, because Casper laps it right up like a good little girl.

"Totally, Meer. That's the entire focus of our channel—paranormal investigations, EVP clips, abandoned exploration, anything that falls under the umbrella of dark tourism. We got you."

Meerkat leans back and relaxes, mentally taking stock of Casper and thinking she looks kind of ridiculous in her overly tight corset with that septum jammed up into her delicate nostrils. Trying too hard.

"So I guess this is the part where I ask the magician to explain her tricks. Cubby and I don't like surprises, obviously. What's the grift on content like this? Lots of editing to make spectral stuff happen? Smoke and mirrors? I don't really care what software you guys use to add creepy effects, just make sure it is effective, 'kay? I have an audience of two million and change, and they see through bullshit."

Casper's brow furrows, and it becomes clear that she's a bit confused.

"I don't mean to alarm you, but we don't edit or doctor any of our footage. We hunt for authentic paranormal experiences. Real and raw interactions with the other side."Meerkat sits for a moment in unreadable silence until Casper becomes so nervous that she fidgets with her chipped purple nail polish.

"We just don't like for our content to be disingenuous."

"Honey, let me school you on something since you're still green. Everything about this fucking influencer gig is *disingenuous*. It's all giggles and kawaii anime eyes when that smartphone is recording, but the moment the camera turns off, fuck those people, fuck their obsession with us, and we sit back and make bank off the performance. It's just acting. We're playing roles here. Now you're telling me that all the ghostly stuff you guys churn out is legit?"

Meer leans forward, and she looks very much like a predatory bird that's about to sink her beak into carrion. Shrewd, dead-eyed, and lacking even a small amount of compassion for the socially anxious girl that sits across from her.

"Did Cubby and I make a mistake linking up with y'all? We don't want lukewarm limp-noodle content, hon. We're not about a snoozefest. The names Meerkat and CubbyWubby are *brands*, and we're only as valuable as the content that we create and distribute. So can you commit to me here and now that we're going to have legitimate spine-tingling freaky deaky shit to stream when the time comes? Nothing underwhelming. Nothing mediocre."

Casper swallows deeply, her eyes drifting to the one of the skoolie's open windows. She drinks in a long breath of midnight air, and some of her composure seems to return.

"I can guarantee you guys will see something otherworldly. We were thinking a midnight séance at an abandoned graveyard about fifty miles outside of New Orleans. With the moon tonight, it'll look amazing in 4K."

Meerkat tilts her head to the side, momentarily intrigued. Something like that could salvage this shitshow of a trip if it's done correctly.

"Any particular spirits we're trying to commune with tonight? Not interested in peaceful grandmothers, kindhearted child ghosts, or lame-ass nobodies. Give me something with a history of violence. Something fucking *juicy*, Casper."

The young vlogger leans back and bites her lip, pausing to push a wind-swept strand of ghostly white hair back behind her ear. Her eyes sparkle in the dark, gold-flecked irises glinting in the gloom.

"Are you familiar with the legend of Hestler Delacroix?"

asper gave Meer the Delacroix CliffsNotes on the rest of that bumpy ride into desolate Louisiana nowheresville. He was a serial killer active about twenty years ago in a few low-income neighborhoods on the outskirts of New Orleans. Hestler claimed seven victims before his reign ended, and his calling card was always dismemberment. Limbs torn from sockets, legs excised at the knee and ankle, digits painstakingly removed with something bordering on artful precision. He was never officially apprehended. It was Hurricane Katrina that took him out, that big boiling monster born of Mother Nature feeding on a lesser human monster. They found him floating dead and bloated in the remnants of his apartment after the disaster, and his cupboards were full of decaying severed arms, his fridge was stuffed with contorted human legs, and he even had a habit of making sculptures from bloody fingers and toes.

There were a few headlines at the time, things like "Dismembered by Delacroix," but with the nationwide attention Katrina was receiving, his posthumous limelight didn't last long. His legend was snuffed out like a forgettable candle before it ever had the chance to truly burn. Remembered by few, and only the most intrepid dark-tourism fanatics like Casper and Binx are left to carry that gruesome torch.

Meerkat and CubbyWubby are following the couple now, the skoolie left behind at the rusted gates of the cemetery, all four of them hoofing it up a hill and into the gaping night. Broken tombstones and hungry mosquitoes greet them, and Meer thinks to herself that this shit had better be worth it. She's expecting a significant boost in her numbers and engagement, and if that doesn't happen, she might burn Casper and Binx just for funsies. Out them as frauds and chop the legs off their channel while it's still a newborn. When you have influence, you have power. That's just the way things are when it comes to existing on the internet.

Meerkat fights against yawns of apathy during the preparation. She's seen enough B-horror films in her life to know how séances go. Casper takes them to a busted up tomb where Delacroix's remains were supposedly interred. It's cramped inside and it smells of mildew, and there are sagging empty bird's nests up in the high corners. Candles get placed, handholding is expected, and Casper takes control of a Ouija board that ends up as their centerpiece on the floor. Meer jostles around, wiping dead leaves from her ass, and she turns on a big bright fake-as-fuck smile for the stream that CubbyWubby has already started.

She whispers to her audience, noticing the comments rolling in too fast for her to be able to acknowledge and read them on the screen.

"It's séance time, guys! Are we ready?"

Casper and Binx take turns saying some suitably cryptic words, aiming to make contact with the spirit of Hestler Delacroix. Meerkat expects Casper to start convulsing and speaking in tongues at any moment, whatever dumb shit they normally do, and she almost welcomes it because it'll spice up the stream and make this exciting. It's been dry so far, and Meer hates dry. Dry leads to the lack of views, and the lack of views leads to the lack of money.

Meer doesn't expect what does happen. She doesn't expect for both Casper and Binx to be seized by some incorporeal force and smashed up through the ceiling of the tomb, their bodies flying up into the night sky with nothing but dust and chunks of stone falling down to choke and gag her and CubbyWubby.

Casper and Binx shriek as they're elevated up into night clouds, but the screams become distant, difficult to hear after a few seconds. Cubby is screaming too, but for a different reason. Something unseen is pressing his face up against a corner of the tomb wall, peppering the back of his skull, his teeth smacking up against the hard surface and falling down bloody against his chin like scarlet-glossed popcorn kernels. There's a popping sound, and his right arm is torn from his body. It is being used to suffocate him, the elbow joint dragging so forcefully against his throat that his Adam's apple caves in and his neck turns limp and wormlike, vomit splashing down against his chest and crotch. At some point he dropped the camera sideways onto the floor, and the stream is still live. Everyone sees.

Everyone sees even when the act of seeing becomes comparable to enduring a snuff film.

Flickers of white noise, and the stream drinks in the cramped confines of Hestler Delacroix's tomb. It is lacquered dripping red, fresh bubbles of hot scarlet. Meerkat sits on the floor, propped up against the wall, still living and staring dead-eyed into the camera. She is armless and legless, just cauterized nubs where her limbs used to be. A helpless nugget of a person, power stripped, influence waning. She waves her stumps for the camera, and this goes on for a full two minutes.

Shit drips out from beneath her skirt, a pool of brown soup, and she has no choice but to sit in it.

She is gargling and spitting and trying to communicate through a brine of pink foam that oozes down past her bottom lip. A vague outline of something that used to be a person paces back and forth in front of her with a disembodied rage that rivals that of Hurricane Katrina. It is snuffing out candles and making dead leaves swirl. Something serpentine and sluglike wiggles on the floor between her dismembered stump legs.

It's Meerkat's severed tongue.

Her eyes are giant terrified saucers spilling over with tears, rivulets of black makeup, and pain. They're all watching her. The comments keep coming. This is a record-breaking stream, the viewership through the roof. She has no tongue to beg them. She has no hand to turn them off.

It is still in here with her, and it is contemptuous and starved and soaked in repressed sadism. It is not done taking pieces from her tonight.

Its *influence* festers and smothers and lords over her in her blubbering snot-slicked final moments, and she moan-mumbles out the word "stop" until all sound erodes into butchery and gristle.

The ghost takes her ears, and it does not stop.

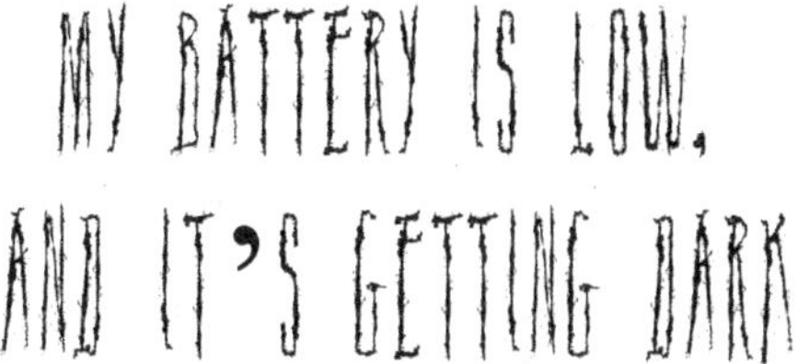

The astronaut sits motionless on a Martian dune, leg folded underneath him, the helmet of his visor a smeared black mirror of nothingness. He should not be here, and his presence makes no sense. It has confounded us and thrown our entire mission protocol out the window.

This is the first manned mission to Mars that NASA has ever been able to get off the ground, and it was meant to be routine. Collect samples, inspect the terrain, and leave a flag planted in the rocky soil to celebrate the hubris of mankind. We're doing what the mechanical rovers before us have done—exploring and collecting data—but this time with actual feet stomping across the gritty red surface of the planet.

We have kept a safe distance from the astronaut, and we've been watching him for hours. He hasn't moved a muscle. His spacesuit is dull obsidian, and it's covered in arcane sigils that none of us can comprehend. We are a group of three: two men and one woman. I am Taylor, there is Robeck, and there is

Malloy. A skeleton crew, and we have sacrificed much to undertake this journey through the stars. We thought we'd planned for every contingency, but we never expected this.

It's clear that the astronaut isn't human. His general shape seems similar to ours, but his limbs are bent at odd angles. His neck is tilted upward, and his gaze seems locked on some distant oblivion. We've sent transmissions to NASA for guidance on how to proceed, but we haven't been able to contact Houston for almost two months now. We believe it is signal interference, so we keep trying. It's not feasible to just stare at this anomaly forever. We've discussed the pros and cons, gone in circles about the topic, and we have to engage. We have to interact. It's possible that the astronaut is dead or that it's just an empty suit with no life-form inside.

I know in my heart that we must approach, but I feel this sense of dread at the thought of doing so. I look to Robeck, and I can see the sweat on his brow beneath his visor. Malloy has been quiet, and I know her mind is full of warring thoughts. We all feel very wrong about this.

I keep thinking about the Opportunity rover and the last transmission that it sent before going offline. All the time it spent exploring this planet, treads crawling along, intent on fulfilling its duties to the end.

That transmission repeats in my head each time I look at the astronaut of unknown origin.

"My battery is low, and it's getting dark . . ."

We are crouched around him, intimately close, and the astronaut shows no signs of life. He does not acknowledge our proximity, and we're allowed to study him in more detail. His suit is similar to Gore-Tex, but the texture it not the same. It looks woven, organic, almost like it was stitched from the hide of some alien undersea animal. The gloved hands have three digits, and those hands are limp in the lap. The helmet isn't terribly different from the ones that we wear, but the visor is tinted and smeared from the inside, allowing no visibility of the face beneath. There's something comparable to an airlock on the neck, and Malloy's fingers tremble close to it. We must, but she's understandably reluctant. Those sigils hurt my eyes. I try to read them and make sense of them, but my vision blurs.

I'm the commander here, so I nod, and she presses against the airlock and twists the helmet upward. There's a hissing sound, like a rattlesnake beheaded and dying in the sand, and then we are staggering back, the helmet dropping from Malloy's hand to lodge in the Martian soil.

The face is wizened, mechanical, and coated in rust and grime. It appears robotic, and judging by the state of the alloy, it has been here for an eternity. A slit for a mouth, and eyeballs just dim turquoise bulbs in deep ocular sockets. We stagger back even more when those bulbs light up, the turquoise brightening, and then the eyes shift to look at us, flakes of rust drifting down from the timeless countenance.

There is nothing we can relate to in that flat gaze. It is apathy, and that is all. Malloy steps forward, finding courage in her gut, and I applaud the woman for her fortitude. She barely even stumbles over her words when she speaks.

"What are you?"

I can't imagine that it'll understand us. We have not the slightest idea of where it comes from or what dialect is familiar to it, but shockingly, the astronaut responds. The voice is a low warble, and it sounds like a machine with a battery that long ago gave up the ghost. A machine running on fumes.

"I am but an emissary. There is one of us for each world in your galaxy. We pave the way for them. They have specific tastes."

My jaw gapes behind my helmet, and I use a vague hand motion to encourage Malloy to continue communicating with him.

"Them? What do you mean, 'pave the way'?"

"I'll show you."

There is a slow clicking from the astronaut's head, old servomotors struggling to function, and then holographic images begin to play in front of its bright bulb eyes. It narrates as it shows us . . .

"Mercury, twenty million years before humanity."

We see lush green jungles. We see large avian creatures flapping through the atmosphere. But how can this be Mercury? It's just a rocky, cratered, uninhabited planet.

We see an astronaut much like the one we are speaking to sitting in a lake full of eellike animals, and then a sequence is triggered. It's like a clock ticking down in the astronaut's head, and once the clock runs down, the jungles explode into mushroom clouds, the lakes are blasted and evaporated, and all life-forms on the planet vaporize.

"Jupiter, sixty million years before humanity."

Bulbous entities float through cities of hydrogen clouds, and they seem incredibly advanced and refined, waltzing through the rings of the planet. An astronaut much like the one before us floats near them, a new arrival, and that same clock sound begins in its head. A countdown to destruction. The cities tumble into dust, and the large floating denizens of the planet explode into gaseous corpse-flesh.

"Mars, five million years before humanity."

Humanoid figures walk across the red terrain, and giant adobe shelters dominate the surface. There is community and culture, and the Martians thrive. Their skin is a glistening red, and their eyes are yellow slits. There seems to be an uproar among them, and they're seen crowding around an astronaut of unknown origin. This astronaut. His clock ticks, and then comes the ruin. Explosions, death, and a planet made barren to the core . . .

The holographic images stop, and we are all left to process what he has shown us. It hurts my head to think about it. All those worlds that we know as empty, dead places . . . they once harbored life and civilizations just like our own?

"Surely you didn't think it coincidence that every world in your galaxy is dead, barren, and empty? It is by design. They *like stillness. They abhor life and noise. They come from a far different place, and a galaxy must be prepared before their arrival. Scrubbed clean, plucked of sentience, and crafted to represent a vast absence. It takes time."*

I can hear Malloy hyperventilating, and she crouches and puts one hand on her knee before the astronaut, digging her hands down into the red soil, trying to ground herself.

"Who are *they?* Why spare Earth?"

Those blue bulbs flicker up, gazing back at the oblivion that only the astronaut seems to see.

"I have been here for long lonely fathoms, and I razed this planet for them lifetimes ago. Nothing to do now but sit and wait. The emissary sent to Earth was late. He was the last. But if my calculations are correct, he should have arrived approximately two Earth-months ago."

Those grinding, broken servomotors start whirring within him again, and we see something we wish we didn't. We see a holographic image of our homeworld. Earth blasted, blackened, and smoking like a cigarette snuffed out on the asphalt. Now it makes sense why Houston stopped responding to us. I hear Robeck screaming the names of his children. I see Malloy stumble and fall, her legs simply giving out from underneath her due to shock.

"If it's any consolation, we took no pleasure. We emissaries are enslaved. Forced. Tools for them. They killed our world too and nested deep in our galaxy. We are just puppets now."

There's a creak, and the astronaut manages to lift up his arm, the material of his suit breaking apart from the sleeve due to how brittle it has become. He points to the starscape behind them.

"Look yonder. Your world was last. They're coming."

Wormholes are bursting into existence beyond the Martian atmosphere, giant knifelike slashes in the fabric of deep space. Shapes are emerging. Enormous god shapes, darker than dark, slithering forth like serpents from holes in the sky. They dwarf the Martian moons; Phobos and Deimos look like thimbles in comparison to the girth of these galaxy killers. They're singing, and the only thing I can compare it to is a mournful whale song. It's strangely beautiful, and the longer I listen, the more my eardrums rupture and bleed. I can barely hear the emissary now. He seems so far away . . .

"I remember the little machine you sent to collect rocks and take pictures. He stayed with me here in the dunes for a time. He was good company before he skittered off, and that little Opportunity rover made me feel less alone on this dead planet. I gave him a message to pass on to your species. I wonder, did you ever receive it?"

The astronaut's eyes are losing their glimmer, that bright turquoise glow flickering out. His head begins to sink down towards his chest. I'm looking at those dark god shapes, watching them eat the stars, and I draw Mallory and Robeck close. I reach out, and I hold their hands. I want us to feel human. And, selfishly, I do not want to be alone.

Their segments emerge from the wormholes, more and more of their body mass becoming apparent, and the longer we watch, the less we're able to stand it. Our brains begin to hemorrhage. I squeeze the hands of my companions even tighter, and I fall to my knees with blood pooling into my thoughts. The astronaut's weakening voice is the last thing that I hear.

"My battery is low, and it's getting dark . . ."

"Ever hear of Handsome Humphrey and the Honey Butter Boys?"

Quint's eyes are gleaming silver dollars in the dark. They're in one of the back rooms of a Baltimore music venue, a cramped dive with cracks in the brickwork of the walls and profane graffiti smeared across windows painted obsidian black. Eviscerated Pelican plays on the ramshackle stage in the main hall, guttural grunts and shrieking animalistic lyrics drifting in from across liminal spaces.

Willow finds comfort here, a hub for the local metal scene, but this band is an opening act for the one she came to see, and she's not too interested in watching their performance. She drifted from the modest crowd, sweaty black-clad bodies and devil horns extended high, and like a background specter, she floated into one of the quieter nooks of the venue to have a smoke.

She stumbled into a little social circle already formed, a gathering of misfits with Quint's blazing Zippo lighter firmly rooted in the center, all of them lounging around cross-legged, sharing cigarettes and other narcotic treats. Willow picks at her black polish, a nervous tic, and she scans the faces around her. All acquaintances, regulars you see at the local shows, but no one she knows on an intimate level. The scene reminds her of an indoor campfire, and Quint is the perfect orator for ghost stories. He's older than the others, but no one can tell how old. She studies his smudged eyeliner, his cadaverous cheeks, and the septum that catches the firelight. All of it like camouflage. His voice reminds her of a crackly radio, and there's a pleasant nostalgia associated with listening to him talk.

She joined the conversation for a particularly intriguing topic. Music that has slipped through the cracks. The history of the dark and obscure, those lost lyricists that are buried in catacombs of infamy. She is familiar with certain tales, but not this one, so, like an eager Nosferatu, she bites.

"Never. What genre? Blues? Jazz?"

A few people murmur, moving shadows in the murk, and Quint shifts his weight while offering up a chuckle. His hand reaches out, long fingers bedecked in silver rings, a menagerie of skulls, serpents, and fanged beasts. He lights his clove cigarette above the Zippo flame, nursing the ember, and Willow follows that tiny red circle with brown doe-eyes.

"If you can believe it, barbershop quartet. Think back to the twenties and thirties. Fancy vests, suspenders, bowties, and dapper straw hats. No instruments, just four dudes harmonizing and uniting their voices as one. Picture it in your mind's eye. A fucking living time capsule in sepia tone."

"What's dark about that? A barbershop quartet sounds about as vanilla as it gets. Eat your Wheaties, say your prayers, and have missionary sex with your wife on a Tuesday night. You're losing me, Quint."

His smirk cracks across his lips, and he shakes his head, gray-threaded dreads framing facial features that could best be described as vulpine.

"We have only scratched the surface, Willow. Patience, young grasshopper, and let the dirty details unfold as they will."

He leans forward and takes a deep drag from the clove-flavored coffin nail, veiny hands dangling between his knees.

"So we've got this quartet, right? Humphrey, Arthur, Pellik, and Junebug. They're as thick as thieves, the kind of brotherhood you can only obtain from traveling the country together, sharing your vocals in cozy little restaurants and at tight-knit celebrations, a camaraderie that evolves from lots of time on the road."

Willow is engaged now, brow furrowing as she flicks ash behind her shoulder into the gloom. The floor lightly vibrates beneath her, drums and guitar and throat-shredding howls creating a background miasma.

"Prohibition hits, and times get tough. Venues aren't booking as often, and Handsome Humphrey and the Honey Butter Boys are living lean and hardscrabble. A few of them have families back home, and they're struggling to provide. Dry towns, thirsty throats, and spirits getting brittle, passion worn down to the bone.

"Somewhere along the way, Handsome Humphrey starts to get a lil' loopy in the head. He tells the others he's been having dreams. Ugly dreams full of tenor and bass. Something that speaks to him through the coalfire of his BBQ pit. The boys catch him sipping rubbing alcohol to drown out whatever nightmares keep boiling through his brain. He tries to tell the boys, mostly in whispers, but they pay him no mind. They think he's just frazzled and spooked because of the financial hardships. Humphrey keeps saying something has been listening to them, and they've stoked an inferno that waits between worlds. Something he calls *Father Furnace*."

Willow is a diehard horror fan and she's desensitized to just about everything, but something about the name *Father Furnace* spoken aloud forces all of the fine hairs on her arms to lift. There's a vile thrum attached to the name. Her imagination runs wild with visuals. Infants burning in their cribs. A flamethrower sweeping the night sky, the melting cheeks of the operator, eyes dripping jelly from the charred sockets. A herd of buffalo stampeding into a wall of endless napalm. She tries to shiver it all away, but the intrusive thoughts don't vacate without protest.

"Arthur steps up and tries to keep the quartet intact. A popular speakeasy reaches out to secure the booking of Handsome Humphrey and the Honey Butter Boys, and it couldn't have come at a more desperate time. Humphrey's nightmares are worse than ever, Pellik and Junebug can barely keep food on the table, and Arthur is at least four months behind on his rent. This is the golden ticket that'll keep their heads above water for quite a while. A big payday for all, and the opportunity to get back on their feet and focus up for future gigs."

Quint sighs, crossing one long leg bedecked in tattered skinny jeans across the other, blowing out his clove-scented dragon smoke into the faces of his eager listeners.

"But Humphrey isn't thrilled about the idea. He says bad omens are in the air when it comes to that speakeasy. His straw hat has started to droop, and it always smells like smoke despite the fact that he's never touched a cigarette in all his days walking the earth. When he stands in front of the mirror to adjust his bowtie, he feels like he's looking into a crematorium, and he sees just blackened sinew and charbroiled flesh where his happy face should be. When he practices his harmonizing, he tastes cinders between his teeth, and no amount of brushing helps him to wash it out."

Willow reaches out, and without even realizing why she's doing it, she starts to swish her fingers back and forth through the flame of Zippo. It's a subconscious thing, and it seems to bring some kind of instinctual comfort.

"Sooner or later, everyone caves, and the show gets booked. They travel into the city that night, get ushered into the secret basement entrance, and take the stage, much to the adulation of the capacity crowd. This speakeasy is a gorgeous sight to see—velveteen sofas, chandeliers, marble pillars, all of it comprising an underground rabbit warren of rooms for social indulgence. The lights dim, and Handsome Humphrey and the Honey Butter Boys put on the show of a lifetime. The old heads that survived still talk about it to this day. The melody enthralled, the bass and tenor were in sync, and the baritone maximized every chord. They ended with an original tune, a longtime favorite, a song called 'She's My Lonely Candle.' And right in the middle of that grand finale, Humphrey pulls a flask from his vest, douses himself in vodka, strikes a match, and sets himself ablaze. He goes up quick, a puppet of clean flame that burns blue, and Humphrey keeps right on singing like nothing at all has changed."

Willow swallows, her throat working. Her mouth feels dry and she wishes she had grabbed some water from the bar, but it's too late to rise up now at this point in the story. Her thirst and her full pulsing bladder will have to wait.

"He burned while his gums bled and his teeth crisped, and instead of running and screaming, his brothers decided to follow his lead. They grasped that flask, one by one, Arthur, Pellik, and Junebug, and they poured that alcohol all over themselves. They self-immolated, and those men didn't stop singing. They were dedicated to their craft. Even as their clothes burned off of them, even as their bowties melted and bonded to their skin, even as they appeared as sloppy staggering rag dolls, a merry band of melting men, their genitals curling up like scorched bits of newspaper, their hair floating off in cascades of ash, their lips peeling up to uncover glistening teeth, Handsome Humphrey and the Honey Butter Boys kept right on singing until the end. Until they were smoking piles of bone in a larger conflagration."

Quint grins, the dancing red ember of his cigarette damn near hypnotizing Willow. It feels like there are no other people in the room but her and him.

"What would cause those men to set themselves on fire like that? Well, I think they were infested. That's the best word for it. Infestation. I think that whatever Father Furnace is, he got into them somehow, starting with Handsome Humphrey. He boiled like cooking oil into their bones, their blood, their hearts, and their minds, and he took them and made them his own. Since it was prohibition times and the speakeasies were designed to be little hidden honeycombs, fire exits were lacking. Seventy percent of that crowd burned in the basement rooms, the barbershop quartet included. Those that fled—smeared in ash and coughing up sludge from their lungs—couldn't seem to get 'She's My Lonely Candle' out of their heads. There are only a handful of records in existence now that include the track. Probably for the better."

Willow takes in a deep breath and exhales a sigh, noticing little tremors in her fingers. She snubs out her cigarette, looking down at it almost distrustfully as the smoke tendril curls outward.

"That's fucking horrible, Quint. What city did it happen in? I've never heard of any of that before."

He shrugs, shining eyes downcast.

"Every city has its tragedies, some slip through the cracks. Gang violence, parks where bodies get dumped and left to fruit. It's easy for bad things to blend together and get forgotten. But to answer your question, Willow . . . right here in good ol' Charm City. The Baltimore beneath your feet."

Quint extends a knuckle, his bony finger pointing downward.

"The charred husk of that speakeasy is right under these floorboards."

Willow feels Quint's unnaturally warm hand on her delicate shoulder, and she allows him to guide her down the stairs, the Zippo held in his other hand, offering only the most paltry illumination. She walks like a zombie with no fixed destination, and she doesn't know why she agreed to this. There's a morbid curiosity in her, and it comes with an ever-present *burn*.

The metal show ended hours ago, the venue is deserted, the doors are locked, and only Quint's relationship with the owner allowed them to have this private sojourn together. They pass dusty barrels, a wine cave, and now comes the door below with melted brass hinges. They enter together, and the aroma is equal parts intoxicating and uncomfortable. Roasted pork left too long to rattle in the oven. Willow inhales deeply, her eyes slitting against the pressure of the atmosphere.

It is a subterranean castle of cinders, contorted bottles, warped sofas, chandeliers that send down snowflakes of ash, and that vague scent of barbecued humans wafting through every sanctified corner. Something is there near the remnants of a ruined stage. Nothing but vapor, a lazy swirling cloud of ill intent, and in that boiling breathing nothingness, Willow sees what the barbershop quartet saw before they elected to burn.

A whisper in her ear from Quint, and specks of saliva that sizzle against her skin from behind wide woodstove teeth. "I was in the crowd that night, Willow. I've been alive a long time thanks to Father Furnace. He put a little flame in my chest, and it won't stop burning."

She sways in Quint's arms, and she imagines what it might be like to skinny dip in a night ocean of gasoline.

Quint sways with her, and he sings in that crackly old radio voice of his.

"She's my lonely candle
When life is blacker still
She's warm in the window
And I watch her always from this distant hill . . ."

ABOUT THE AUTHOR

Jeremy Megargee has always loved dark fiction. He cut his teeth on R.L Stine's Goosebumps series as a child and a fascination with Stephen King, Jack London, Algernon Blackwood, and many others followed later in life. Jeremy weaves his tales of personal horror from Martinsburg, West Virginia with his cat Lazarus acting as his muse/familiar. He is a native of Appalachia and you can often find him peddling his dark words in various mountain hollers deep within the wilderness.